CASSANDRA

ROMANCING A GOD SERIES

CHARLEY MARSH

TIMBERDOODLE PRESS

INTRODUCTION

Cassandra was the daughter of King Priam, the last king of Troy, and Queen Hecuba–so technically she was Princess Cassandra. Like all story princesses she was extraordinarily beautiful.

The god Apollo courted the lovely Cassandra and bribed her with the gift of prophecy if she would only sleep with him. (It's never a good idea to sleep with someone you have to bribe. They're either attracted to you or they aren't.)

Cassandra agreed to Apollo's offer and accepted the gift but then refused to go to bed with him. Apollo was understandably upset with Cassandra's rejection. Unfortunately a divine power once given cannot be taken away so Apollo took his revenge by ordaining that Cassandra would continue to see the future but no one would ever believe her warnings.

Life went downhill after that for Cassandra and she was eventually murdered. Depressing. I've chosen a different story for Apollo and Cassandra, a modern take with a happily ever after.

CHAPTER 1

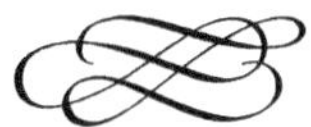

CASSANDRA BROWN WHIPPED her ancient Toyota 4Runner into the boatyard's parking lot and headed for the employee's parking area at the far end.

A collection of upscale vehicles already dotted the lot: high dollar SUVs mixed with Mercedes, Cadillacs, Audis, and BMWs, the status symbols of the boat owners who wanted to get in an early sail or time on the water before heading off to their swanky offices in the city.

Cassie pulled into the empty slot between her boss's new Tundra and her friend Amber Day's almost-new Volvo wagon, smirking over the mental picture of her 4Runner as the thorn between two roses.

The music cut out abruptly when she turned off the engine. Although she was already late she sat and listened to the cooling engine's pings and pops.

She rarely listened to tunes at an ear-splitting volume, but she had spent another late evening with her fiancé and his mother and was having trouble waking up. The loud music, while irritating, helped.

Cassie swallowed the last of the still warm coffee in her travel mug and stepped out of the 4Runner. An onshore breeze hit her face immediately, bringing with it the smell of frying donuts from the small waterfront cafe that opened early to accommodate the boaters who hadn't thought to bring something to eat or drink with them.

Her mouth watered at the smell of fried dough and sugar. She had slept through her alarm so hadn't had time for breakfast. Unfortunately, as Jonathan had already scolded her twice last week for tardiness she had no time to grab anything now either.

Cassie pulled her heavy tool bag from the passenger seat and slammed the door. It bounced open and she slammed it again. She didn't bother locking it. There was nothing of value inside and the 4Runner was by far the crappiest vehicle on the lot. No one would ever try to steal her car—one of the few bennies of being perennially poor.

The tool bag was a pain to lug back and forth every day, but it had been one of the first things she'd made for herself when she'd made the switch from sailmaker to canvas worker and it held practically everything she owned of value.

Constructed of tough navy blue denier on the outside and lined with heavy white canvas, the bag boasted numerous pockets and slots for everything she needed to do her job. A heavy duty zipper ran along three sides and allowed her to spread the bag flat for easy access.

It was the most deluxe of tool bags and a fine example of what she was capable of creating, if she did say so herself.

More important, all of the tools inside the bag belonged to her—not the marina—a fact she took pride in. She'd had to save for each and every tool and build her collection slowly, always researching carefully and buying the best quality tool she could find.

Cassie shifted the bag to her other hand. She could have left the bag in the sail loft each night—Jonathan swore no one would mess with it— but she couldn't do it.

To appease Jonathan, who kept harping on it,

Cassie had tried leaving the bag in the loft one night. After a sleepless night worrying about her tools she vowed never to leave it again. Pretty much all of Cassie's net worth lived in her tool bag, so she hauled it between work and home.

And she had to admit that if she decided to leave Portland suddenly she would need the bag of tools to start a new life. She hoped that this time she could stay—she always hoped that she could stay—but something always seemed to happen that forced her to pull up whatever shallow roots she'd managed to put down and move on.

She hoped that after the last move she'd learned to keep her mouth shut. No one needed to know that she had visions. Especially not now, not when she was on the verge of forever distancing herself from her lowly beginnings.

The sight of the boats moored in the marina filled her with happiness, especially the ones wearing her canvas. *Her* canvas. Conceived, designed, built and installed by her own hands.

Cassie took her canvas craft seriously and was beginning to build a reputation in the Portland area as a conscientious and skilled fabricator.

It helped that she was female and treated her customers well—unlike the men who owned the area's three other canvas shops. The demand for canvas far outran the supply and the other shops tended to be arrogant, with a "We'll get to you when we get to you, take it or leave it" attitude.

This spring, for the first time since she had started working at Haskell's Marina, people came asking for her specifically. Instead of just asking Jonathan if the sail loft handled the specialty canvas items people liked to buy for their boats, they actually asked for Cassandra Brown.

She couldn't be more thrilled.

Smiling now, Cassie stepped onto the covered walkway that ran the length of the south side of the long, cedar-shingled building and headed for the double doors that opened directly into the sail loft.

The walkway protected customers headed to the marina offices, or Mike's Chandlery—where they could buy everything and anything a boat owner could possibly want—or to Bounty of the Sea, the marina's popular seafood restaurant that looked out over the protected bay that was home to the marina.

The middle of June meant the boating season was in full swing. Portland's boaters wasted no time once winter released its icy grip on Maine's southern coast. The boating season was short and the enthusiasts were dedicated to making the most of it.

Despite being late, Cassie stopped a moment to enjoy the sight. Beyond the large marina building the bay sparkled in the morning sun. Hundreds of white hulls bobbed on their moorings. Sailboats of every size and design, power boats, and fancy sport fishing boats gently rocked and slowly spun in the gentle breeze.

Cassie saw the Boston Whaler the marina used to ferry the boat owners back and forth carefully weaving its way through the moored boats. She squinted at the helmsman. Broad shoulders and sunlight glinting off shiny dark hair told her that Pauli was working the launch this morning.

Good. She needed a ride out to a customer's boat for a fitting as soon as she gathered her things. Of the three launch drivers she liked Pauli best. The other day driver, Amos, was very nice, but there was just something special about Pauli. He had a way about him, an ease with people that she envied since she seldom felt easy around others.

Cassie stopped just inside the sail loft doors to remove her deck shoes and tossed them to the side with everyone else's. The entire sail loft floor was their work table and had to be carefully protected from dirt and scuff marks. Customers were allowed no farther inside than the door, a policy that was fiercely and gleefully policed by the sail makers.

It wasn't often one of the ordinary citizens got the chance to scold and reprimand the wealthy class. They enjoyed it so much that Jonathan had been forced to create a rotation sheet ensuring that they each got a turn.

Cassie loved working in the large, open loft. Bright and airy, with windows on three sides that let in the light and sea breezes, it was a pleasant and inviting space that could easily have held four apartments the size of her own.

Constructed of plywood sheets covered with a dozen coats of polyurethane, the scrupulously clean floor gleamed in the morning sunlight. Five sewing machines were the only obstructions on the bare floor.

The stitchers sat in wooden boxes suspended below floor level, only their torsos and arms visible. The often massive projects were laid out on the floor where they could be moved around and fed through the machines with a minimum of hassle.

It was the nicest sail loft Cassie had ever worked in.

"Morning, Cassie." A heavy-set man in his late twenties called to her from his knees where he was carefully cutting a large sheet of white dacron with a heat knife.

A black symbol stuck onto one corner told her he was working on a new sail for the J series of racing boats that were popular in the area. Most sailmakers added any lettering and numbers at the end; Stan liked to buck the trend and put his on first. He claimed they helped him tell which end was up.

"Hi Stan. How's it going?" Cassie skated across the floor in her thick socks over to the corner that housed her canvas projects.

"Oh, you know. It's going. Jonathan was looking for you earlier. Did he catch you?"

Cassie's heart sunk. There were only two reasons her boss would seek her out: either a customer had a problem, or he wanted to give her another warning about being late.

"Thanks. No I didn't see him. I have to do a fitting once I grab my stuff. Can you tell him I should be back in about two hours?"

"Can and will," Stan replied.

The image of a bewildered Stan standing in an

empty apartment flashed into Cassie's mind. Poor Stan. He was a truly nice guy. It sucked that his wife was planning to leave him.

She pushed the image aside. Past experiences had taught her that sharing her visions would not change things. If anything, sharing with Stan would destroy the friendly working relationship that she had going with the man. People didn't appreciate the bearer of bad news.

She forced her brain to concentrate on what she needed for the fitting. The launch operators didn't appreciate it when she had to make extra trips because she forgot something.

Her boss Jonathan liked it even less.

"Every trip costs the marina in wages and gas," he had lectured her the one time she had forgotten to stock her bag with a special fastener the customer had requested. "The next time this happens I'll deduct both from your week's pay."

Cassie had made sure it didn't happen a second time. She needed every penny she took home.

She pulled the cut lengths of blue Sunbrella fabric from their slot and checked the customer name, boat name, and supply list she had clipped to the end.

Originally constructed from tightly woven

cotton, modern day canvas was a synthetic that stood up better to the constant wear of salt and sun. Cassie would've preferred to work with cotton canvas, but her customers were educated and wanted the latest hi-tech fabrics.

"You headed out?" Amber Day, sailmaker and friend, called to Cassie from her sewing box. Lightweight yellow, green, and blue fabric billowed around her upper body. By the end of the day the fabric would be stitched into a complex design, taped and grommeted; a completed spinnaker soon to be seen flashing around the Casco Bay islands.

"Yeah, I have a dodger fitting," Cassie answered. She pulled boxes of snap fittings from a cubbyhole and put them in her bag. Five boxes: two parts to the snap cap, two parts to the snap stud, and one of screw-in studs that attached to the boat. Check. Snap tool. Check.

"Little late getting going, aren't you?"

Cassie looked up at the slight snark she heard in Amber's voice. Since Cassie's engagement last month to Brad Farland III, Esquire she had felt a small wedge in their friendship. She inspected her friend while she wondered how to deal with the growing distance between them.

Amber had pulled her frizzy red hair back in a

tight ponytail. Her large green eyes, filled with hurt resentment, looked back at Cassie from a pale, freckled face.

The resentment bothered Cassie. She made every effort to behave as she always had, despite her recent engagement to Portland's most eligible and wealthiest bachelor. She decided the best path was to ignore Amber's snark.

"The wine-tasting went later than I thought it would and I couldn't leave until Brad did. I wish you had come with us. Brad wouldn't have minded."

Amber snorted. "Yeah right. What about Brad's mother? Somehow I'm sure that Portland's most famous society dame would have minded a great deal if you brought an unapproved guest to her shindig."

"You're not—" Cassie stopped. The bitter truth was that Charlotte Farland, queen of Portland society, *would* have minded if Cassie brought Amber with her to the charity tasting.

"Yeah, that's what I thought." Amber bent her head to her sewing machine and fed the flowing fabric through with skilled hands.

Conversation over.

Cassie hurriedly pulled the rest of her supplies

together, put her deck shoes back on, and headed for the dock to catch the launch.

Being engaged to Brad wasn't working out quite like she had thought it would. Instead of expanding her circle of friends, it seemed to be having the opposite effect—the number of real friends, a small one to start with, was shrinking.

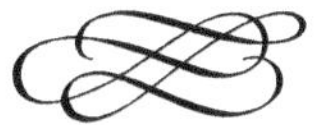

CASSIE KEYED in the combination to the marina gate and carefully pulled it shut behind her. The gate prevented trespassers from accessing the long dock and the boats berthed along its twenty-four short finger docks.

Boat owners paid top dollar for the dock berths. There was no waiting for the launch to ferry them to their boats. No rowing a small skiff out to their mooring. The Chandlery and restaurant were near at hand. Even landlubbers could enjoy being aboard a boat when it was securely fastened to a dock.

Cassie walked the length of the central dock toward the large platform at the end where boaters could buy gas and ice without leaving their watercraft.

She ignored the owners enjoying coffee in their deck chairs unless they spoke to her first. That was a hard and fast Haskell's Marina rule. It was even in the employee handbook. *Rule Twelve*: "Do NOT speak to the boat owners unless they address you first."

Being the friendly sort she had questioned the rule. Didn't it make more sense to offer a cheerful "Good morning" to someone?

Now that she had met Brad's mother Charlotte Farland and her peers, she understood the wisdom of the rule. Some people considered themselves too precious to be addressed by the lowly working class.

She reached the gas/launch dock and set her bags down with a sigh of relief. The drawstring canvas bag that held the fabric pieces for the fitting—called "blanks"—was nearly as long as she was tall and kept getting tangled in her feet.

Fortunately she had installed the stainless steel tubing frame that would support the dodger yesterday so she wasn't trying to juggle that as well. Sometimes working canvas on board a rocking boat felt a bit like being a one-armed wallpaper hanger.

She half-sat on one of the round-topped pilings that customers tied up to and pulled on her dark glasses and pith helmet against the sun's glare. Like skiers on snow, anyone who spent time on the water knew how the water's surface reflected the sun's rays. Sunburn was an occupational hazard that Cassie tried to avoid.

She breathed in the salt-scented air and smiled. She loved the ocean.

Several minutes passed before she heard the gentle drone of the approaching launch's outboard engine. She saw that Pauli had two passengers with him and moved her stuff off to the side where they couldn't possibly trip over them and then complain that it was her fault.

Pauli cut the engine and the launch drifted toward her. The launch's hard rubber fenders bumped softly against the platform's edge. He tossed her the bow line and she quickly secured it, then walked aft to catch the stern line.

A middle-aged couple holding travel mugs sat in the boat waiting for Pauli to give them permission to disembark. Cassie could smell the enticing aroma of hot coffee rising from their mugs and wished she had some too.

The woman, trim and gray-haired, smiled at Cassie and wished her a good morning. The gentleman smiled at her as well as he gave his wife a hand up to the dock. They wished Pauli a good day and hoped they'd see him when they returned from a trip into Portland and headed up the dock.

They had barely reached the midpoint when a trio of teenagers came racing down the dock and nearly knocked the wife into the water.

"Wait! Wait for us!" yelled one of the boys.

Cassie had been about to hand Pauli her tool bag. She started to pull it back.

"Give it here," he said, grabbing for the bag. "Those rude kids can wait a minute or two."

"Oh, but the customer always comes first," Cassie said in a whisper, trying to pull the bag back without much success.

"Those young pups need to learn some manners." Pauli managed to get her bag and set it at his feet. "This is the third time this month they've come running and shouting down the dock, expecting me to drop everything to accommodate them."

Cassie glanced back at the three. The two young men looked like brothers. Dark hair, same athletic build, nearly identical attractive faces. The slim blonde with them was obviously not related.

Skipping school? "Shouldn't they be in school?" she asked.

"Probably. I have a feeling Daddy doesn't know they're sneaking girls out on his cigarette boat. That's the third different girl they've brought out this month."

"Oh. Huh. I hate those cigarette boats. They're so loud and obnoxious."

"Yeah, well that pretty much describes the males in that family. The boys come by it naturally. Hand me your other bag and step aside— here they come. They'll knock you into the water if you don't watch out."

"Pauli, my good man," said one of the brothers. "Take us to our boat. We don't have much time, so chop chop."

Chop chop? Cassie rolled her lips to hold in a laugh. The kid was doing his best to act like a big man and impress the girl. She cut her eyes toward Pauli, watched his eyes go flat.

Expressive eyes, Cassie noted. Pauli had the most beautiful blue eyes. A deep, clear blue that currently reminded her of the cold waters of Casco Bay on a sunny winter day.

"I am no one's *good man,*" Pauli said, his deep voice deceptively mild. "Help your friend into the launch, please."

Both brothers reached up and grabbed the blonde's hands and pulled her into the launch. She landed on the younger brother's lap and giggled when he wrapped his arms around her.

Cassie refrained from rolling her eyes although she really, really wanted to, and untied the stern line. Pauli restarted the motor as the stern floated away from the dock. She untied the bow line and tossed it into the launch, then leaped lightly after it, landing next to the older brother.

He immediately put his arm around her and pulled her down into his lap. His hand slid over her breast. "Good thing I caught you or you would have gone right over."

Cassie glared at him as she pushed to her feet. Customer or not, the boy had no right to grab her like that.

"I know how to get in and out of boats," she said coldly. She curled her hand into a fist to keep from slapping him. "I don't need your help. Lay a hand on me again and you'll be sorry."

The blonde tittered and the boy flushed red. Cassie made her way to the stern and sat next to Pauli.

"You okay?" he asked. He had watched the brother pull Cassie into his lap—and watched him cop a feel of her breast while doing it. The trio now had their heads together and were oblivious to Pauli and Cassie.

"Yeah. Arrogant idiot," Cassie said quietly. "My least favorite kind of fool. I'd like to dunk him in the bay, but hey, you know, *customer*." She smiled.

Pauli smiled back. He liked Cassie. He liked women in general, but he was learning that Cassie stood a cut above the average female.

She had it all as far as looks went; thick, chestnut colored curls that were presently tied back and bouncing below a very stylish woven pith helmet, and warm large brown eyes with golden highlights that fairly glowed when she was pissed—like now. He liked that her wide full mouth tended toward smiles more than frowns.

She might be on the small side—petite was the term short women liked to use—but she had plenty of curves packed onto that tiny frame.

But that wasn't the best part about Cassandra Brown. She was not only intelligent without having to show it off, she was kind and compassionate. Pauli was a sucker for kind and compassionate.

And if all that wasn't enough, what really intrigued him was the sense that Cassie was hiding something. Something big that she didn't share with others. A secret that he meant to dig out if he got the chance. Truth was one of his cornerstones.

He watched Cassie without seeming to as he headed toward the outer ring of moorings.

Cassie watched the water as Pauli guided the launch skillfully through the moored boats to the southern end where the motor boats were kept. The two boys were noisily vying for the blonde's attention, but she had finally noticed the handsome launch driver and she couldn't take her eyes off Pauli.

And who could blame her? thought Cassie with an inward grin. Pauli was an incredible specimen of the male half of the species. His navy blue Haskell's Marina polo shirt stretched across his broad chest and brought out his blue eyes.

His khaki shorts exposed his tanned, well-developed legs and hugged a very nice butt. And his face, his face looked like it had been chiseled by angels.

She tore her thoughts away from Pauli's physical attributes when the launch pulled up next to a long, low cigarette boat painted fire engine red.

The boat was exactly what Cassie had expected—a giant phallic symbol painted so nobody could miss it. She jumped up and grabbed the edge of the cigarette boat's hull and pulled the launch close. The rubber bumpers hanging off the sides of the launch prevented any damage to the hull paint while the boys and their guest crossed from one boat to the other.

"We'll need you to pick us up at eleven sharp," the older brother said. "Don't be late."

He hurried to the helm and switched on the big engines. They came to life with a powerful roar.

"Fool," Pauli said angrily. "He was in such a hurry to impress the girl he didn't even take the time to empty the bilge of built-up fumes. He could've blown us all to kingdom come."

Cassie stared at the cigarette boat while the launch pulled slowly away. In her mind she saw the blonde leaning over the side sicking up. The boys were not going to have the fun they expected this morning. Their passenger would soon be seasick.

"I suspect you'll be picking them up well before eleven," she said without thinking.

Pauli looked at her, curious. "Yeah? Why do you say that?"

"I, uh, I just meant that the girl doesn't look like a boater to me." Why had she spoken her thoughts aloud? This was how she always got in trouble. She looked around for a new subject.

"I'm headed to Jerry Fowler's sailboat, the *Sea Maid*, mooring number four seventy-six. I figure two hours to do the fitting. Will you tell whoever's driving the launch to pick me up then?"

Pauli narrowed his eyes at Cassie. A small spark of *knowing* tugged at him. There was something there. Something vague and undefined in the background, but *something*. She had sounded so sure about the kids coming back early.

He wanted to dig deeper but suspected that Cassie would clam up on him so he kept silent. One lesson he'd learned well was how to bide his time.

"I'll still be on," he answered. "I'm running a double today so Amos can pick his wife and daughter up from the airport."

Cassie pictured the tall, skinny Amos who always had a smile and a joke for her. "That's nice of you. Where did his wife go?"

"Visiting her family in the midwest. Fly over country." Or it would be if his older brother Zee hadn't just married and settled there.

Zee's marriage was partly responsible for Pauli's presence in Maine. The brothers were close and had always traveled and hung together, played and dated together.

Without Zee, Pauli felt off. Not quite himself.

He had stopped dating and was driving the launch—a mindless job—while he figured out what he wanted to do next with his life.

Cassie was a nice distraction from his personal problem. She gave him something new to think about. A puzzle to unravel. Pauli enjoyed puzzles.

"That's the one." Cassie spotted the gleaming stainless frame she had installed on the Fowler's boat. She pointed and Pauli set the launch against the boat's hull.

Without her asking, he tossed the heavy tool bag onto the sailboat's deck as if it weighed nothing while Cassie held the boats together. Her bag of canvas blanks followed.

Grateful for the help, she grabbed the *Sea Maid's* deck rail to haul herself aboard, but before she could Pauli placed his large, strong hands under the cheeks of her ass and boosted her onto the deck as if she were a child.

"All set?" he asked as the launch drifted away from the sailboat.

Cassie swallowed and lowered her head so the pith helmet hid her flushed face.

"I'm good. Thanks," she called with a wave. She waited until he was lost amid the boats before she let herself sink to the deck.

Holy Crap. Her bottom still felt the heat of his hands through the thin khaki fabric of her shorts. His touch had sent an unexpected zing through her body that still had her shaking.

Cassie shook her arms and hands, trying to dispel the energy. She was engaged to Brad for heaven's sake. She had no business reacting to another man's touch, especially if that man was a co-worker. It was common knowledge that love affairs between co-workers were disasters in the making.

Love affair? Good lord, what was she thinking! She and Pauli were nothing more than co-workers and acquaintances. She barely knew the man. Nor did she have any desire to know him better. Pauli was a summer hire, here for the season and then on his way.

Besides, given how she'd witnessed nearly every woman who came into contact with the handsome launch driver openly drool over him, she'd hazard a guess that Pauli had access to more women than he could handle.

She shut off her thoughts and turned her attention to the job at hand.

If Pauli could've heard Cassie's thoughts he would have laughed. He wasn't blind. He saw the come-hither looks that women gave him, but he had some hard and fast rules when it came to dating.

No married women, ever. No exceptions. And no virgins. He wasn't a heartbreaker. He preferred to date women who were looking for a short term good time and were unaffected when he moved on and out of their lives.

Did an engaged woman count as married? he wondered as he maneuvered the launch next to the dock. His palms still tingled from the feel of Cassie's firm, round bottom. He hadn't expected that. He had given her a boost the way he would have boosted a child or his sister.

Cassie had *not* felt like either one.

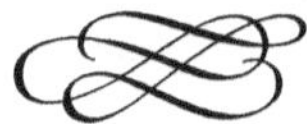

CHAPTER 3

CASSIE RAN her fingers up and down the stem of her wineglass and wondered why she had agreed to have dinner with Brad tonight. She was exhausted, too tired to even keep track of the conversation.

She tried to rally her energy. She was having dinner with the man she loved, just the two of them. An elegant dinner in Brad's elegant home. A home that was a far cry from the tumbled-down, peeling shack that she'd grown up in.

An elegant home that would become her home after the wedding.

She looked across the white-clothed, polished cherrywood table set with fine, thin china, crystal glasses, and real silver flatware and took in the always pleasing sight of her boyfriend Brad.

Fiancé, she corrected herself. Brad had asked Cassie to marry him two weeks ago and she had said yes, despite the nagging fear that they were ill-suited because they came from two such different worlds.

Had it only been two weeks since they'd become engaged? It felt much longer ago than that. There'd been so many must-attend events since the announcement in the paper that Cassie felt as if they'd been engaged for months. No wonder her friend Amber was feeling neglected.

She picked up the wineglass and took a small sip of the very expensive red whose name she'd already forgotten and let her gaze wander around the room.

The trappings of the Farland family wealth greeted her everywhere she looked: from the thick, hand-knotted Persian rug beneath her feet (Brad had told her precisely how many knots per square inch but she'd forgotten). A rug with a deep blue background, which apparently was more desirable and more valuable than the red background rugs.

Old, gilt-framed oil paintings hung on the pale blue, silk-covered walls.

She averted her eyes from the still life paintings of dead rabbits and birds, the matched scenes of hunters on horseback with hounds chasing a doomed red fox across the English countryside.

Everything in the room was in its place and there was a place for everything—as long as it was worthy.

Cassie wondered where she was meant to fit. Would she be expected to—

"Cass? What do you think?" Brad, classically handsome Brad, the Farland golden boy with his perfectly cut, sun-kissed brown hair and hazel eyes, his straight nose, square jaw and gym-toned perfect body, was looking at Cassie expectantly.

Lordy, what had he been talking about? Cassie flushed and set down the wineglass. She really needed to pay closer attention. She didn't want Brad to think she was a scatterbrain.

The whirlwind of social engagements that she had attended recently with Brad and his mother had completely worn her out. How did they do it night after night?

Practice, Cassie decided. Brad and Charlotte Farland had grown up in the life. Attending social functions that lasted late into the evening several nights a week was their normal. Would she ever grow used to it?

"Whatever you think is best, darling," Cassie said aloud. To her relief Brad smiled.

He reached across the table and took her left hand—the one now sporting a huge square cut yellow engagement diamond—in his.

To Cassie's discomfort, the diamond seemed large enough to be used as an emergency beacon. She had tried to refuse it, claiming that it was too much—too *ostentatious* for a simple girl from the poor section of the city she wanted to say, but didn't. Brad had insisted that "all the Farland brides wear the family diamond."

Cassie had clearly heard what wasn't said. "If you want to be a Farland, you do as the Farlands do."

To be part of the elite one must play by the elite rules. Her father would have been tickled pink to see his little girl move into the upper ranks of society from lowly Gorham's Corner.

She saw no point in telling Brad that she kept the diamond safely hidden away, only putting it on when she saw him.

As far as the other changes, she supposed that she'd get used to the social engagements. It was like training for an athletic event, right? She had to build up her strength and stamina, hone her skills at small talk and fake smiles.

Brad was definitely worth the adjustments she found herself making. Once she knew all the rules and how to play by them she could break a few and make her own mark on the family.

Brad ran his thumb over the diamond, a gesture of pride and ownership, and smiled at her.

"That's great, Cass. You'll make Mother very happy."

Make his mother happy? What had she just agreed to? She didn't have to wait long for the answer.

"Mother and Father had their wedding reception at the country club forty years ago," Brad continued. "It's a family tradition."

One reception does not a tradition make, Cassie thought with an inward frown. A mental image of hundreds of people dressed in their very best finery popped into her brain.

Uh-oh. Now was not the time for a vision. She tried to box the image out but the mental movie reel continued to roll. She heard the dull roar of a powerful engine, saw a sleek black motorcycle pull up to the open double wide door of the building holding all the people, and knew that catastrophe was about to strike.

"Cass? Where'd you go?" Brad squeezed her hand.

Cassie gave a little shudder and the spell was broken. The waking dreams had started when she turned thirteen—that magical age when fiction writers loved to bestow their characters with special powers.

Only in her case the dreams served no function other than to alarm people when she tried to warn them of pending trouble.

She forced a smile. "I'm right here. I was just wondering how many guests you and your mother will be inviting to the reception."

Brad relaxed and dropped her hand. He forked up a flaky piece of fish en papillote before answering.

Why couldn't they just call it what it was? Cassie wondered as she took a bite of her own. Why did the rich have to have fancy words for everything? Fish poached in paper. Poached fish. Big deal. Even the most impoverished fishing family knew how to wrap fish and bake it.

The first time Cassie had eaten the poached fish with Brad's mother Charlotte, Charlotte had sternly corrected Cassie that it was *not* simply baked fish and insisted that she learn to pronounce the French correctly.

"Pah-pee-yote," Charlotte had chided. "Repeat after me." Charlotte had reminded Cassie of Miss

Foulette's seventh grade French class—a class she had failed miserably. Once again she forced her thoughts back to the present.

"Around four hundred," Brad said after carefully wiping his lips on his linen napkin. He set the napkin beside his plate and picked up his wine. "Mother has decided four hundred is the perfect number to make invitees feel special. Intimate while still making a statement."

Cassie blinked. "Four hundred? Your mother thinks four hundred guests is intimate? Brad, I thought we agreed on a small wedding. I told you I wanted to keep it small and you agreed."

Anger mixed with a sense of helplessness created a knot in Cassie's chest. She put down her fork. She was determined to like Brad's mother but the woman had a warped view of the world.

Brad reached across the table and squeezed Cassie's hand again. "Don't worry, sweetheart, we kept the ceremony small. Mother culled the reception guest list from over a thousand potential names and she's limited the number allowed at the ceremony to two hundred."

A thousand guests! Four hundred sounded almost reasonable compared to that number. And only two hundred of Brad and Charlotte's nearest and dearest business associates at the ceremony, thought Cassie with an inward sigh of resignation.

There would only be her co-workers representing her side.

She thought of the black motorcycle and felt the edge of panic begin to move in again.

"Are you all right? You seem awfully quiet tonight." Concern showed in Brad's eyes.

He really was a good man and she was a lucky woman. Cassie had never thought she'd rise above her poor background. To have a man like Brad love and want to marry her was a dream come true.

Making his mother happy made Brad happy. The wedding was only one day after all. She could deal with it.

Cassie shook her head. "I'm just tired tonight, that's all. It's been a long week and the wine tasting last night ran later than I'd planned on. I'm not used to a full social calendar."

She smiled. "If you don't mind I think I'll skip dessert tonight and go home. See if I can catch up on my sleep."

"Of course, darling. Don't worry, you'll soon get used to it all. I'm sure thinking about the wedding has also been keeping you up these past two weeks."

Brad carefully wiped his mouth again, neatly folded his napkin, and stood. "Don't you worry your pretty head about any of it. Mother will take care of everything."

Cassie followed Brad's example although she didn't understand why she should fold a napkin that was headed straight to the laundry room.

Brad led the way down a wide hallway to the back door. Tiffany style wall lamps cast a soft, colored glow on the polished oak floor. Several family portraits done in oil by local artists graced the hall walls.

Cassie wondered if her portrait would be added to the family gallery. It felt odd to think of someone painting her picture.

The hall ended in a large, wood-paneled mudroom with a tile floor that held a center drain. Two antique oak deacon's benches flanked the entry door. Cassie sat on one and exchanged her Birkenstock sandals for sneakers, popping the sandals into her tote bag.

The sandals weren't appropriate footwear for a formal dinner, she knew. When Brad had asked her to join him for dinner tonight she had pictured an intimate evening with pizza and beer on the couch in front of the big flat-screen t.v., not crystal and china in the formal dining room.

She gave him credit for not chiding her on her choice of clothes even though she'd caught his slight frown when he saw her faded jeans and loose sweater. Next time she'd ask about the dress code and not assume, she promised herself. She had so much to learn.

Brad lifted Cassie's worn jean jacket from the coat tree and helped her into it, then turned her and wrapped his arms around her.

"You sure you're okay? Not having second thoughts about getting married, are you?"

Cassie warmed at the concern in Brad's voice. She shook her head. "No. No second thoughts. Like I said, I'm just tired tonight. Lack of sleep and I worked outside on a couple of boats today —all that fresh air always makes me sleepy."

Brad pulled her against his chest and nuzzled her hair. "After we're married you can quit that job. You'll have plenty to do as Mrs. Brad Farland the Third to keep you busy. You won't have time to work on other people's boats."

A small bubble of panic began to rise in Cassie's chest. She pulled away from Brad and searched his face.

"You know I love my job, right?"

"Sure. But we'll have plenty of money. And you'll have social obligations to fulfill. Mother will help you with all of that."

A small frown line appeared between Cassie's delicate eyebrows. "I'd like to keep working, Brad. At least until we start our family." She smiled at him, a mischievous gleam in her eyes. "Hopefully that will be right away."

"We'll have plenty of time to have children, Cassie. You'll be kept busy, I promise."

Cassie shrugged off Brad's obvious reluctance to start a family right away. She wanted children—as many as possible. She was tired of being alone in the world. A large family would mean she'd never be alone again. Brad would change his tune once he held their son or daughter in his arms.

"Kiss me good night." Brad pulled her close again and kissed her. When he lifted his head his eyes glittered.

"I'm looking forward to our wedding night. Drive safely, Cassie." He opened the back door and stepped outside with her.

The security lights lit up the fancy pale yellow cobblestoned parking pad and the four car garage that was larger and finer than the average middle class home.

Cassie pushed down a sense of disappointment and walked to her car. Just once she wished Brad would get swept away by passion and take her to his bed, but he always acted the gentleman. She supposed she should be grateful he wasn't an animal.

She gave an audible sigh of relief when she'd shut herself inside her old, familiar 4Runner.

What was wrong with her? She must truly be tired, she decided. Brad was a wonderful man. A real catch according to the local magazines and every woman she'd met since becoming engaged to him. Her life was a fairy tale dream—poor girl meets rich boy, falls in love and lives happily ever after.

She was just feeling overwhelmed at how much she had to learn and become used to. Learning Brad's world was like being dumped inside a foreign country where she didn't know the customs or the language.

If only her future mother-in-law weren't quite so . . . rigid and controlling. Charlotte had yet to show any real warmth toward Cassie. Oh, she was unfailingly polite and said the right things, but Cassie always had the feeling that Brad's mother seemed to be assessing her.

And yet Charlotte had seemed genuinely

pleased when Cassie accepted Brad's marriage proposal.

Well, she wasn't going to figure out Charlotte Farland tonight. Cassie started the engine. The lights flicked on, passing over the large maples and oaks that ringed the house and garage. Brad's place was set on a prime piece of real estate, high on a wooded hillside overlooking the Atlantic Ocean.

Cassie wondered if she'd be able to put in flowers once she lived here. She loved flowers, especially the spice-scented rugosa roses that grew wild on the coast.

She saw that Brad stood in the doorway waiting for her to leave. She tooted the horn on her way down the drive and saw him go inside. She knew he hated her old Toyota. He had offered to buy her a new one but she'd put him off, insisting that he wait until after the wedding.

She loved her old beast. She had scrimped and saved until she had enough to buy it without a loan. Like the bag of tools, it was hers and hers alone.

What would Brad say if he knew about her visions? Charlotte would probably recommend a lobotomy and an extended stay at some pricey sanatorium. Cassie shuddered at the thought.

She pushed aside the question that had nagged at her all day. Why had the brief touch of Pauli's hands on her body excited her far more than Brad's kisses ever had?

CHAPTER 4

THE NEXT MORNING Cassie rolled into the parking lot on time. She had an inside day scheduled and was looking forward to stitching together the new dodger for the Fowler's boat.

Sewing relaxed her. Watching the flat canvas blanks take shape as she fed them through the machine gave her tremendous satisfaction. When finished she would have a three-dimensional object that provided protection from the salt spray, wind, and sun.

"Morning, Stan. Morning, Amber. Where's Jonathan?"

"Staff meeting," Stan answered. "He's going to ask for another sailmaker since he's being called out to deal with customers all the time. We're backed up on sails and he's too busy to sit and sew all day. We need a stitcher drone."

"Don't look at me," Amber grumbled. A neat stack of red and white spinnaker cloth sat to her right. Several lengths had already been pieced together and billowed in a colorful cloud in front of her. "I have all I can do to keep up with these."

"And you do a great job." Jonathan came into the loft and kicked off his shoes.

Average height, average looks, with a sailor's tan; Jonathan did not stand out in a crowd the way Brad did. Cassie liked him immensely. He was what her father would have called "salt of the earth." A hard-working, honest family man with a lovely wife and two young boys who were the center of his world.

"Do we get a new stitcher?" Cassie asked from her sewing box. She carefully stitched around the second porthole window on the dodger wings, being careful not to catch the protective paper.

"Yes. Brenda's placing an ad in the Portland paper today. Hopefully there'll be someone out there who started job hunting late."

While Jonathan, Cassie, Amber, and Stan worked through the winter, the sail loft didn't take in enough work to keep them busy full time.

Few boat owners thought about their boats in the off season.

Consequently the bulk of their orders came in the late winter through midsummer. The new hire would be a temp and laid off as soon as the work slowed, an ideal position for a college student.

The morning passed pleasantly for Cassie. Sunshine and fresh air filled the loft. It was her day to choose the music and she had Count Basie playing.

The sewing machines hummed and raced. The dodger went together smoothly, thanks to a careful fitting and the marks she'd learned to put on to insure the curved pieces stitched together without puckers.

By late morning she had stitched on the white dacron edge tape that gave extra body for the fasteners and helped prevent the dodger from prematurely wearing. The signature diamond-shaped Haskell Sail Loft label followed.

She gathered up the dodger and padded over to the handwork corner to install the grommets and fasteners.

"Looking good," Stan said. "I'm headed to Farrell's Market for an Italian sandwich for lunch. Can I pick you up anything?"

"Ooh, yes. Good idea. I haven't had an Italian in weeks. No onions, extra black olives and napkins. I think I'll dine on the Fowler's boat and install this baby this afternoon. Thanks, Stan."

Forty-five minutes later Cassie sat in the stern of the launch with Pauli, her tool bag, and the carefully wrapped dodger at her feet. She kept the paper bag holding her sandwich in her lap to protect it.

The launch was full. Fortunately they were divided into only two parties and were headed to two large sailboats moored close to one another. It didn't take more than twenty minutes for Pauli to drop them off and deliver Cassie to the *Sea Maid*.

Pauli tossed the launch's bow line over the sailboat's rail and transferred the dodger and Cassie's tool bag to the *Sea Maid's* deck. He turned and held his hand out, wiggled his fingers.

"Hand me your lunch. I'll pass it to you after you climb aboard."

"I can manage," Cassie said. She didn't want to part with her sandwich. The smell of it was making her mouth water. She just wanted Pauli to leave so she could enjoy her meal.

"You wouldn't want that Italian sandwich to fall into the water, would you?"

Cassie's eyes narrowed suspiciously. "How do you know I have an Italian sandwich in here?"

Pauli's smile lit up his face and eyes and made Cassie's blood thrum. No mortal man had the right to be so attractive.

"I can smell it," he said. "An Italian sandwich has a distinctive odor. Yeasty bread, cheese, olive oil, green peppers, tomatoes, hard salami." He sniffed the air and squinted at her. "You skipped the onions. Shame on you. They're part of the whole Italian sandwich experience."

"They give me onion breath," Cassie mumbled.

"Come on, hand it over." Pauli's hand reached out.

Cassie reluctantly handed him her sandwich bag, then climbed onto the *Sea Maid* before he could boost her up.

To her surprise, Pauli followed her.

"What are you doing?" she asked as he moved easily into the sunken cockpit.

Pauli nodded toward the launch. "The radio's on. I'll hear if someone needs me. It's lunchtime and I'm hungry. I'm hoping you'll share that sandwich."

Share? She had planned to eat half and take the remaining half home for dinner. Or maybe even eat it all now.

"Please? You wouldn't let a co-worker starve, would you?" Pauli batted his thick black eyelashes at her and smiled.

"Oh, very well. You can have half," Cassie grumbled.

"Great." Pauli sat in the cockpit and patted the seat opposite. "Let's eat. I really am hungry."

Pauli ate quietly and neatly. He stretched his legs across the cockpit and set his feet on Cassie's seat, near to her but not quite touching, and lifted his face to the sun.

Eventually he felt her relax and he smiled inwardly. She was a guarded little thing. Always a little tense, as if waiting for something to happen. If she could relax with him this close then she must trust him at least a little.

Cassie cautiously stretched her legs and set her toes on the opposite seat, careful not to touch Pauli. She bit into the oil soaked bread. The sun warmed her bare arms and legs. The boat rocked gently in the small swell, waves quietly slapping the hull, lulling her. Seagulls sliced through the clear blue sky overhead calling to their mates.

"You enjoy your work." Pauli broke their silence as he licked his fingers, then wiped them carefully with the napkins Cassie had shared with him.

"I not only enjoy it, I love it. It's challenging and satisfying. I love solving the puzzle of how do I create something practical and utilitarian, and at the same time make it attractive? Most of the boats I work on are sleek and beautiful and I believe their canvas has to convey that same feel."

"From what I hear you succeed at the challenge. Quite a few of my passengers point out your work and comment on how fine it looks."

Cassie blushed. She felt absurdly pleased by the compliment. Her work was out there for all to see, and to hear that people thought well of it mattered a great deal to her.

"That's really nice to hear. I don't get much feedback in the loft. Sailmakers tend to look down on canvas workers. The sails are the important thing because without them the boat won't move. The canvas . . ." she held her right hand out and flipped it back and forth . . . "a frivolous afterthought. Like putting those colored sprinkles on a really yummy, thick-frosted cupcake."

She looked at Pauli, curious. "How do you know they're pointing out *my* work? It could come from one of the other local shops."

"I can see the difference. Plus your label. Your pieces are perfect, or darn near. No wrinkles, no flapping, no sloppy installation. The lines are clean, sleek and smooth. Quality all the way. Some of the canvas I see should be dropped overboard it's so bad. You can tell whoever made it took no pride in their work. They didn't care. You care, and it shows."

"You understand. I'm a little surprised. And strangely pleased."

A wide grin split Pauli's face. He nudged Cassie with his toe. "What? You thought I was just a gorgeous face?"

Cassie laughed and stood. "I need to get this dodger installed. Thank you for inviting yourself to lunch. I enjoyed the company. You know how to be quiet and I appreciate that in a companion."

"We'll do it again soon. I'll buy next time. *Two* sandwiches."

Pauli leaped lightly into the launch and headed back to the dock with a wave.

Cassie found herself smiling several times that afternoon. The installation proceeded smoothly and by late afternoon a beautiful white-trimmed, navy blue dodger graced the *Sea Maid's* cockpit. She called Pauli to let him know he could pick her up when it was convenient and gathered her tools.

"Looking fine," Pauli said as he helped Cassie into the launch. "Sit in the stern with me. I have to pick up the same people we dropped off earlier."

Cassie settled in as Pauli skirted the moorings toward his pick-ups. Even though the longest day of the year was approaching and the sun hung high above the islands to the west, the breeze off the water had grown cool. She pulled a faded sweatshirt from her tool bag and pulled it on, then settled in to enjoy the ride.

The sailors they picked up were in high spirits after an afternoon of cocktails in a nearby cove. Cassie couldn't help but notice that several of the women worked hard to catch Pauli's eye. One particularly striking blonde flipped her long hair and shimmied her ample chest in his direction.

Cassie looked up at Pauli to see if he had noticed. He looked down at her and winked. Embarrassed, she ducked her head, stretched her legs, and crossed her arms over her chest.

Of course Pauli had noticed. How could he not? The woman was practically throwing herself at him. Had the blonde no shame? She wore a large diamond with a wedding band. What if one of her companions told the woman's husband that she was trying to seduce the launch driver?

Cassie did a mental eye roll. She took commitment seriously and expected others to do the same. But she knew that many people didn't.

They reached the dock and Cassie leaped out to secure the lines. She stood to the side and watched Pauli help those who needed it out of the launch. Several of the group were obviously tipsy.

The blonde tottered and fell back against Pauli. His arm went around her and she turned into him, pressing her body to his. Pauli placed his hands under her elbows and lifted her to the dock as if she weighed no more than a child.

Cassie hid a smile at the woman's pout. But as the blonde followed the others up the dock, Cassie had a flash of a BMW off the road, rolled over in a ditch, the blonde's bloody face behind the wheel.

She raced after the woman and touched her arm. "Be careful on the drive home. Maybe you should get someone else to drive you." Too late, she saw several people sitting on the nearby boats, watching and listening.

The blonde glared at Cassie and yanked her arm away. "Are you trying to say I'm drunk?" she demanded loudly. "You have no right. Who do you think you are?" She stalked up the dock, leaving Cassie staring after her with a sick feeling in the pit of her stomach.

She *knew* that the blonde woman would have an accident on her way home. Knew it to the bottoms of her feet. Nobody ever believed Cassie when she tried to warn them. And why should they? No sane person went around telling others she'd had a vision, *and oh by the way*, don't go here, or don't do that, or, or...

"What happened there? Why did you do that?" Pauli stood on the gas dock with Cassie's tool bag and the empty canvas bag that had held the *Sea Maid's* dodger.

"I, uh, . . ." What could she say? "It's obvious the woman had too much to drink and shouldn't drive. Look at the way she fell into you. I was just trying to help her. Obviously I shouldn't have said anything."

She held out her hand for the bags. "I'll take those. Thanks for your help. I'll see you around."

"Not so fast." Pauli kept the bags and looked down at Cassie. "Something happened there. You got a glazed look in your eyes and seemed to disappear for a few seconds, then you went chasing after that obnoxious blonde."

Cassie's breath caught. It was bad luck that Pauli had noticed the brief lapse. She had to bluff him into thinking he hadn't seen anything.

"You're mistaken," she said, reaching for the

bags. "The light must have caught my eyes wrong. Give me my bags."

Pauli looked down at her, his expression thoughtful. "Now that I'm thinking about it, the same thing happened when we dropped those kids off at the cigarette boat. You told me I'd be picking them up earlier than they'd asked for and you were right. So what gives, Cassie Brown? Do you have *the sight*?"

Fear clutched Cassie's stomach. She was happy here, had made a place for herself. If rumors started circulating that she experienced visions it would all fall apart. She'd be forced to start over. Again. No one wanted to work with a crazy woman.

"Don't be ridiculous," she said with a disdainful sniff. "Anyone could see that young girl had no experience with boats. It was an observation—a lucky guess. I'm tired. I want to clock out and go home. Please give me my bags."

Pauli frowned but handed over Cassie's bags and wished her a good night.

She headed up the dock on shaky legs. Her vision of the accident had been very clear and strong. She always felt a little weak afterward when they were strong like that.

But that wasn't all that was giving her the

shakes. Pauli had guessed her secret. If he mentioned her visions to anyone else people would start asking questions.

If Brad or Charlotte heard about her visions what would Brad do? Surely the prim and proper Charlotte would never welcome a psychic into the family gene pool.

Cassie reached the head of the dock and turned back toward Pauli as she normally would. It was important to behave normally. It was something she had struggled with soon after the visions had started.

At the time she had carefully watched the other girls her age and copied their mannerisms so she would blend in. Blending in was important. When she blended nobody noticed that she was different.

Pauli stood at the end of the dock, still watching her, the puzzled frown still on his face.

Cassie gave a quick wave and smile and fast-walked out of sight before he decided to come after her with more questions.

CHAPTER 5

CASSIE STOPPED by the sail loft just long enough to drop off the empty canvas bag and punch her time card. It had been a long couple weeks. Too many late nights with Brad and busy days with the canvas. She felt exhausted and was looking forward to a quiet evening at home with a book and a glass of wine.

"Long week?" Amber came up behind Cassie and stabbed her time card into the clock. The old-fashioned clock gave a loud 'clunk' as it printed the time on the card. Amber slid the card into her slot on the metal rack.

"Yeah, too long." Cassie gave Amber a thoughtful look. "I could use some girl time.

Would you be interested in wandering around the Old Port tomorrow? Maybe hit a few of the funkier shops and grab some lunch?"

Surprise flashed in Amber's eyes and was quickly hidden. She shrugged. "Don't you have plans with Brad?"

"Nope. I'm on my own and looking forward to a free day. How about it? I'll even treat lunch."

"Free lunch? In that case, sure. It's not like I have anything better to do. What time and where do you want to meet?"

Ten minutes later Cassie let herself into her apartment. Built nearly a century before over the garage of a once-wealthy estate, the space suited her perfectly.

Despite only living there for two years, the apartment felt more like home than anywhere else she had lived. After several years moving from marina to marina she had finally managed to carve out a place for herself here on the southern Maine coast.

The main room of the apartment was large and open, with soaring posts and beams and windows on three sides that looked out either over Casco Bay or the expansive, wooded estate grounds.

She unlocked the heavy oak door and with a loud sigh set her tool bag on its mat where it would sit for two blessed days. She hung her backpack on its wooden peg and leaned down to pick up her cat; a fat, emerald-eyed, gray tortoise-shell she had found the previous summer, skinny and abandoned in the marina parking lot.

"Hi, Handsome," she said, rubbing her face in the cat's soft fur. Handsome bumped his head against her chin and purred in response.

"It's just you and me tonight, fella, and I couldn't be happier."

She padded the length of the room to the small alcove that housed the kitchen area. Handsome meowed loudly in anticipation when she opened a can of salmon-flavored cat food—his favorite. Cassie flaked it out onto a pretty yellow-flowered plate and set the plate on the floor.

Although relatively small, the kitchen was well-appointed and efficiently designed. It lacked a dishwasher, but Cassie made so few dishes she preferred to hand wash them anyway, so that was no big deal for her.

She pulled a pot of chicken and wild rice soup from the fridge and set it on the gas stove to heat, then reached back in and pulled a bottle of chilled sauvignon blanc and poured herself a generous glass, adding three ice cubes.

She knew that Brad and Charlotte would shudder with revulsion at the idea of adding ice to wine—such a classless thing to do to good wine!—but Cassie liked her whites to stay cold and she didn't mind the slight dilution.

She wandered over to her dining table set in front of one of the large windows that looked toward Casco Bay and stood sipping the wine.

Decompressing. Letting a week's culmination of stress from creating the perfect canvas for picky boat owners slide away.

It took several minutes and half the glass of wine before she began to relax and feel at home.

She turned away from the window to look at her apartment and sighed with pleasure. Like her other furniture, the worn oak dining table was a second-hand store find.

Cassie rarely bought anything new. She preferred the used and loved, pieces with history and character. She enjoyed the search for what she needed and preferred to do without until she found the right piece.

Because of that, her living space was eclectic and homey. No sleek chrome and glass living or dining room sets for her. She liked funky and different.

The square oak table with its five extra leaves had been exactly what she wanted. With its thick plank top and heavy, fluted legs, it took up very little room until the leaves were added. Then it easily seated sixteen.

Since she only had six chairs (and no two matched) she had yet to invite sixteen for dinner. Not to mention that she didn't have sixteen friends to invite. But still, the potential was there. Cassie believed in potential.

She set down the wine and headed for her bedroom loft. Built over the kitchen and bathroom alcoves, it was accessed by an open oak staircase that ran up the wall nearest the bathroom.

She pulled off her clothes and tossed them to the floor below before grabbing her favorite worn sweats and heading back down the stairs for a shower.

Picking up the discarded clothes, she shoved them into the full laundry hamper. She really needed to get caught up on household chores this weekend. No excuses.

The washer and dryer were located in the bathroom, taking up space that might have been used for a tub, but as she'd rather have a washer and dryer than have to deal with a laundromat, Cassie considered it a fair trade.

She stood under the hot shower with her palms braced against the 1940s black and white tiled wall, the water as hot as she could stand it, and washed away the salt and fatigue. She groaned out loud when the knots in her shoulders loosened slightly.

As she toweled dry the image of the blonde with her face bloodied rose unbidden in her mind's eye.

The vision on the dock had left her shaken. Unlike the one a few days ago with the seasick girl, this one had foretold serious injury. Those were always the worst ones—the visions that told her someone was about to get hurt.

"There's nothing you can do about it, Cassie," she mumbled. She had tried to warn the woman at the risk of being reported for rudeness toward a marina customer.

Cassie's warnings had cost her other jobs at other boatyards. "She's rude" and "she's crazy" were the complaints heard most often. She didn't blame her employers for letting her go. They had no choice. She needed to learn to keep her mouth shut and her visions to herself.

She'd thought she had control of it, but given what happened with the blonde today, apparently not.

Shower finished, Cassie dressed in her faded navy sweats and thick, wool socks. She combed out her hair and left it. It would dry in a riot of thick curls, but she didn't have to tame it for anyone tonight. She could relax and be herself, one of the bennies of living alone.

She checked her soup, adjusted the heat, set the timer, and returned to her wine. No television tonight, she decided. She had a good JD Robb murder mystery to finish.

She turned on the compact disc player and cued up Diana Krall. The singer's husky contralto voice came through the speakers and Cassie lowered the volume to keep her in the background before settling on her couch with the wine and her book.

Handsome leaped onto the couch, curled up at her hip, and began to wash his immaculate fur.

The phone rang just as the kitchen timer buzzed, startling Cassie. Lost in her story, she had forgotten all about the soup.

And that's why you set the timer, Cassie girl, she thought as she raced into the kitchen to silence the angry buzz.

Timer silenced, she ran across the great room to the door and pawed through her backpack for her phone. Why did she always have to carry so much stuff? She finally gave up and upended the pack so everything fell out at her feet.

She kicked through the assortment of hair restrainers, notebooks, pens and pencils and markers, tape measure (in case she came across an interesting piece of furniture and needed to know its dimensions), granola bars, crusher hat, emergency tampon, empty water bottle, and her latest philosophy read. Finally she glimpsed the dark reflective screen of her phone.

"Yes? Hello?" Cassie sat on the floor with the phone on speaker and began to replace all the junk back inside the pack.

"Cass? Did I catch you in the shower?"

"Oh, Brad, hi. No, I was in the kitchen and then I couldn't find my phone."

"Well, if you carried a regular pocketbook instead of that ratty backpack you wouldn't have that problem."

Cassie quickly squelched the wave of irritation at Brad's comment. Backpacks, foreign to the upper class women he usually dated, were an item he equated with college students.

"Are you kidding?" She managed a chuckle.

"Have you seen the size of some of those pocket-books women carry? You could hide a baby elephant in them. Besides, I like to have my hands free."

Cassie finished loading the last hair tie into the pack and stood up. "So what's up?" she asked before Brad could get going on the subject of handbags and fashion. "I thought you were dining with your mother tonight,"

"I am. Mother is thrilled that you agreed to hold the wedding reception at her club. She called her friend who manages the event center to make an appointment for us to work on the details and Mavis said she could squeeze us in tomorrow morning. She had a cancellation and put Mother ahead of several others on the waiting list." His voice held a slight hint of triumph in it.

Cassie's stomach clenched. "Brad, I'm sorry, but I have plans for tomorrow. It would be rude for me to cancel them now." Not to mention that cancelling would add another brick to the wall that Amber had begun building between them since Cassie had begun dating Brad.

Cassie heard Brad say something to his mother. She couldn't believe he was calling her with his mother right there. Cassie could picture her future mother-in-law's eyes narrowing at the thought that someone would dare mess up her careful plans.

What about Cassie's plans? By all rights they should have checked with her before committing to an appointment that included her. Without realizing it Cassie straightened her shoulders, readied for battle.

"Cassie? I'm afraid you'll have to cancel. I'm sure whatever you have planned can wait. This is important to Mother. Mavis Franks is a *very* busy person and she's doing Mother a huge favor by squeezing us in. I'll pick you up at ten."

"Brad, no. I can't cancel." Damn that Charlotte Farland. The woman was so used to everyone doing things the way she wanted. Brad's mother seemed to have no inkling of the concept of compromise. Everything was win or lose to her.

"Cassie," Brad hissed. "You *have* to cancel. You don't understand what a big deal this is. Mother *asked a favor.* Now she *owes* Mavis Franks. She can't just call her back to say 'Never mind.'"

Why not? thought Cassie obstinately. What made Charlotte Farland so special? Everyone else in the world had to eat crow occasionally.

"Cassie? I'll pick you up at ten."

"No. I'll meet you there." She ended the call

without saying goodbye. It was childish, she knew, but it made her feel better.

Too frustrated to sit and read now, she scooped herself a bowl of soup and turned on the television. As she flipped through the channels she stopped on the local news when she caught a shot of a car upside down in a ditch.

The camera zoomed in on a figure being loaded into the back of an ambulance. A moment later a head shot of a pretty blonde flashed on the screen.

"Oh no." Cassie let her spoon fall into the bowl of soup as she scrambled for the volume.

". . .The driver, Melody Harbush, wife of prominent Portland attorney Donald Harbush, was apparently returning from an afternoon spent with friends when her BMW went off the road. Police are questioning two witnesses who claim they saw the accident."

Cassie sat frozen.

Melody Harbush. The same blonde who had flirted with Pauli that afternoon. The same blonde in her vision. The woman she had tried to warn—had been in a car accident.

Cassie turned off the television and set down the soup bowl. Her stomach felt too knotted to eat any more.

She had tried to warn the woman. She had done what she could, but still a familiar feeling of failure swept through her. She had a gift, a gift that nobody but her took seriously. Not for the first time, she wished she'd been born in ancient times. At least then people believed in fortune tellers and seers.

CHAPTER 6

"AMBER, HOP IN," Cassie called across the front seat of her 4Runner to her co-worker.

Amber climbed into the vehicle and snapped on her seatbelt. "I thought we were going to wander around the Old Port? Where are we going?"

"We are. But first I have to do something for Charlotte Farland. I thought you might want to come with me and I could use your company. It shouldn't take long."

Cassie swung into traffic and headed back the way she'd come. She hadn't been able to bring herself to call Amber last night to cancel their plans. This morning she had decided that since Charlotte insisted on dealing with reception plans this morning she would just have to put up with Cassie's friend.

It occurred to her now that another reason she hadn't cancelled her plans with Amber was because she wanted a buffer between herself and her future mother-in-law.

And possibly Mavis Franks, a woman she knew was cut from almost the same cloth as Charlotte. Almost but not quite, because Ms. Franks worked for a living.

Cassie concentrated on not hitting any of the tourists who spilled off the old brick sidewalks onto the Old Port's cobblestone streets. She skipped the Arterial and opted for the Eastern Promenade instead because she loved the view.

Set just below the eastern crest of Munjoy Hill, the view from the promenade over the harbor was magnificent. The gray granite stone of Fort Gorges, a remnant of the days when forts were still being built to safeguard the coast, anchored the middle of the deep blue harbor.

Several hazy blue-green islands dotted the horizon beyond the fort. A half-dozen sailboats, their white sails billowing, already plied the waters between the islands and Portland. The water sparkled with millions of pinpoints of light. Black-tipped gulls wheeled beneath puffy white clouds, their raucous calls filling the air.

Runners dressed in a variety of get-ups, from neon to ragged sweats, ran along the promenade. Children, carefully watched by parents who downed steaming cups of coffee from go-cups, played on the sloping green. Dogs chased frisbees and tennis balls. Teens hung in groups and tried to look as if they cared about nothing.

It was a typical weekend morning in one of the city's premier parks.

"Well? Where are we going?" Amber asked. Her eyes narrowed. "I hope you're not taking me to the boatyard. I've had my fill of that place for the week, thank you very much."

Cassie coasted to the end of the promenade, turned right onto Washington Ave, crossed the bridge, and shot up Route 88 into Falmouth.

"Brad called last night," she said, keeping her tone light. "Charlotte made an appointment with the woman who runs the event center at her country club to talk about the wedding reception. She didn't realize I had already made plans for today. It shouldn't take long, really."

"You're taking me to the country club?" Amber hooted. "This should be good. You see what I'm wearing, right?"

Cassie eyed Amber's paint-splattered farmer's overalls and tight, faded green tee.

"You look fine. Love the overalls, by the way. They look really comfy."

Amber didn't speak again until Cassie pulled her old Toyota into the club's parking lot. She wove through rows of shiny new Mercedes, Beemers and Audis, until she found an empty slot.

Well-manicured lawns with strategically placed trees, flowering azaleas, and beds of tulips and daffodils surrounded the lot and clubhouse.

"It's even worse than the marina parking lot," Amber observed as she climbed out of the 4Runner. "Are you sure this is what you want? To have your wedding reception, a big deal event, here—with hundreds of strangers?"

Cassie shrugged. "It doesn't matter. If it makes Charlotte happy that makes Brad happy. I'm doing this for Brad."

"Hmmmm," was all Amber said in reply.

They walked up a wide curved path paved with crushed clamshells and edged in purple pansies to the double-door entryway and let themselves inside the stone and glass building.

They found themselves in a large foyer decorated in dark wood panelling. Wide oak floorboards gleamed between thick, red Oriental rugs. Comfortable looking leather chairs were placed in small intimate groups around low glass tables topped with colorful bouquets of fresh flowers.

The windowed wall opposite the doors looked out over the club's highly-rated golf course. A stone fireplace dominated the wall to the right. A fire snapped and crackled in the hearth, breaking the sudden silence.

A woman who appeared to be their age got up from one of the chairs and hurried over to them on sky-high skinny heels. Nattily dressed in snug white sailor pants and a navy sweater that emphasized her large, obviously artificial bust, her long, pale blond hair hung straight to her midback.

Cassie felt herself bristle as the woman approached.

When the blonde reached them she shook her hair back and looked primly down her nose at them. "I'm sorry. This club is for members only. You'll have to leave."

She wasn't a bit sorry. Cassie could tell the woman took great pleasure in telling them they didn't belong there. Story of her life. She didn't really belong anywhere. That didn't mean she was going to let this blonde bitch get away with dissing her and her friend Amber.

She made her voice as cool and haughty as the blonde's. "I'm here for a meeting with Charlotte Farland and Mavis Franks. Could you please point me toward Ms. Frank's office?"

Surprise followed by curiosity flickered through the woman's pale blue eyes. She pursed glossy red lips as if she wanted to call Cassie a liar, then shook back her hair again and negligently pointed to their left with a red-tipped finger.

Red, white, and blue. How patriotic of the bitch.

"Down that corridor. Can I tell Mavis you're here to see her?"

"No. Thank you." Cassie strode off with Amber quietly chuckling at her elbow.

"I'll bet there's a lot more of those where she came from," Amber said when they were out of earshot. "She might even be a guest at your reception."

"Bite your tongue. Unfortunately places like this are always full of people with nasty attitudes. Something about the narrow gene pool, I think."

Amber sniggered. "Or maybe they're trained

to be that way. I see the office. Let's get this done and go have some fun."

Mavis Frank's office door opened into a medium sized reception area. Her personal assistant, a thin—was thinness a prerequisite to work or belong there?—woman dressed in a plum colored skirted suit with matching high heels, led them into the event coordinator's office and offered coffee or tea which they both declined.

Mavis Frank's office was paneled in the same rich dark wood, with oak floors and a thick oriental taking up most of the center of the large room.

Six deep and cushy chairs upholstered in dark brown leather sat in an intimate seating arrangement around a low, glass table to their left. Mavis's massive oak desk gleamed with polish and anchored the right side of the room. A vase of fresh white peonies sat on one corner.

Apparently even the employee's spaces kept up the theme of no-expense-spared-for-our-members.

Mavis herself turned out to be another tall, thin, and coolly efficient female. Cassie felt a tightness in the back of her skull that she knew would soon bloom into a headache.

They sat and made small talk until Brad and

Charlotte showed up, offering no excuses for being ten minutes late.

A subtle power play, Cassie deduced. By being late, Charlotte was asserting her place in the hierarchy. Mavis held an important position in the club, but bottom line, she was nothing more than hired help.

Charlotte had asked a favor which put her in the untenable position of owing an underling. Arriving a few minutes late shifted some of the power back to Charlotte by reminding Mavis Franks that she was the employee and Charlotte the boss.

No wonder Charlotte had refused to cancel the meeting. It would have undermined her position even more. Inwardly Cassie shook her head over what she considered silly power games.

Charlotte wasn't pleased when she saw that Cassie had brought Amber. She inspected Amber's clothing with barely concealed revulsion.

"Perhaps your friend would like to wait in the reception area while we speak with Ms. Franks," Charlotte said.

"Amber will be fine, I'm sure," Cassie answered, keeping her tone light. "And she might have some good ideas to contribute. Shall we get started?"

"I had thought we would dine in the club after our meeting," Charlotte said to Cassie with a pointed look at Amber. "There's a dress code."

Cassie gave her future mother-in-law a bright smile. "I appreciate that, Charlotte, really I do, but Amber and I had already made plans for today and I couldn't reach her to cancel."

The lie rolled easily off her tongue. "Let's see what we can accomplish in the next fifty minutes before I have to leave," she continued. There. She'd put Charlotte on notice that she only had an hour and Charlotte had already squandered ten minutes of it by showing up late.

She ignored the slight frown that passed over Brad's face. If he knew her at all he had to realize that Cassie would never allow his mother to coerce her into something she didn't want to do—unless it was something that didn't matter.

"Yes, let's start, shall we?" Mavis Franks hit several keys on her computer. "You want to reserve the large event hall. When do you need it?"

"September fourteenth. And yes, I realize that it's short notice but my son would like to marry this fall," Charlotte answered.

Mavis Franks' gaze flicked to Cassie's abdomen.

She thinks I'm pregnant! Cassie realized. She

flushed and opened her mouth to speak but before she could say anything Charlotte spoke again.

"It's not what you think, Mavis." There was no mistaking the ice in Charlotte's voice. "Brad is up for partnership in his firm and they prefer that their partners be settled. We've simply moved the wedding date up to ensure that Brad doesn't have to wait another year to make partner. You understand."

Mavis nodded. Her long-nailed fingers moved quickly over her computer keyboard. She frowned. "It doesn't look good, Charlotte. As you're aware we usually require a year's notice to reserve the large hall for an event of this size. Mid-September is only twelve weeks away."

She shook her head and swiveled away from the computer to look at Charlotte. "I don't think we can accommodate you."

Cassie saw Charlotte stiffen from the corner of her eye. She hadn't known her future mother-in-law long but she already knew that Charlotte expected to get her way. She waited to see how Brad's mother would handle this.

"I noticed at the last board meeting that you had put in a request for new drapes for both the large and small event halls," Charlotte said. She picked a piece of non-existent lint from her immaculate suit. "Very expensive drapes, if I'm remembering right."

Mavis's expression turned stony. "The ones we have are looking their age. I'm simply trying to maintain the club's image. That's part of my job."

Charlotte nodded. "Of course, of course. And the board appreciates your efforts, we really do. But the cost of replacing those drapes—how many are there? Fifty in all? And they're extra long so I understand they will have to be custom made. You've decided on Belgian linen?"

Cassie turned her attention to Mavis and saw the club manager's eyes narrow. What was Charlotte getting at? Cassie wondered.

"Yes," Mavis answered. "The Belgian linen will not only look luxurious, the drapes will wear well and hold up for many years. I believe it is the most cost effective option, although it will take a significant outlay."

"Yes," Charlotte agreed. "That will be a huge expenditure for the club to absorb. I believe your estimate came in at close to one hundred fifty thousand dollars."

Cassie heard Amber's sharp intake of breath. She felt a little awed herself. One hundred fifty thousand dollars just for drapes? She could buy a decent house for that amount.

"What is your point, Charlotte?" Mavis had a wary look in her eyes.

Charlotte looked at Mavis, her gaze steely. "The board has already agreed to find a way to fund the new drapes. However, it's such a large outlay I believe we will have to suspend any raises or bonuses for at least the next year, possibly two."

She paused a beat. "Unless the Farland family was willing to make a substantial donation toward the drapes. Say, fifty thousand? Do you understand me, Mavis?"

Mavis looked as though she had something unpleasant stuck in her throat. She swiveled back to her computer and tapped the keys again.

"Martin Schumann reserved the large hall on September fourteenth for his company's yearly meeting. I'm sure I can convince him that the smaller hall will be more than adequate."

Charlotte smiled. "I appreciate it, Mavis. Now let's get down to details."

Charlotte dominated the remainder of the hour with an occasional "What do you think, Cassie?" thrown in. Cassie went along with whatever the two women suggested. She found that she honestly didn't care. The wedding reception was for Charlotte and her vast number of "friends."

The wedding and the life afterward were for her—her and Brad.

What did it matter whether the name plates they used at the tables to identify guest seating were bronze or silver framed?

Cassie listened with growing horror as Charlotte worked out an insanely expensive menu and briefly discussed the seating needed for the various politicians, judges, and other members of the bar who would attend.

Charlotte arranged for token gifts for each guest to be set on a table near the door. Silver bags with a black stripe containing a tube of expensive moisturizer for the women and a black with silver stripe bag holding a pass for a round of golf at the club for the male guests.

Apparently all the men played golf.

Cassie jumped back in when it came to the cake. "I want square tiers, six layers, chocolate, with alternating raspberry cream and marshmallow cream in between the layers and chocolate buttercream frosting."

Amber made a yummy noise.

Charlotte shook her head. "Nobody has a

chocolate wedding cake, Cassandra. Or a square cake. We can do the six layers but we 'll go with the traditional round, white cake, white icing. It's what people will expect."

"Than maybe it will be a nice surprise for them to be served something unexpected. My wedding cake will be square and chocolate," Cassie insisted.

There would be no compromise on this, she determined. She had wanted a square, chocolate wedding cake forever—since she had learned that's what her mother had made for her own wedding.

"We'll leave the cake for later," Charlotte said. "We don't need to settle everything now. We have the event hall booked, number of guests, menu, and table settings, and gifts for the guests decided. That's enough for today."

Fifteen minutes later Cassie and Amber were speeding back to the Old Port.

"How do you put up with her?" Amber asked. "She's like—" she shuddered—"she's everyone's worst nightmare of a mother-in-law. A skinny ogress who dresses in expensive clothes and wears pointy shoes."

Cassie laughed. "You aren't far wrong. Mostly I ignore her. Charlotte's going to do what Charlotte wants to do. I put up a fight when it's important to me. The rest I let her have what she wants. Keeps the friction to a minimum that way."

Amber's red hair bounced around her face as she shook her head. "Better you than me. I'd be butting heads with the witch over everything. I can't believe she wouldn't let you have the cake you wanted."

"Oh I'll get my cake, don't you worry. *That's* important to me. We'll have a chocolate cake." She glanced at her friend. "Thanks for coming with me. It wasn't really fair of me to spring it on you like that but I appreciated the company."

"It's always interesting to see how the upper-crust does things. Lots of fake-ass hoity-toits in places like that. You do realize that once you marry the Third you'll be hanging out with lots of people just like the blonde who tried to toss us out of the club?"

"The third?"

"Yeah, you remember, your fiancé, Bradford Farland III?"

Cassie laughed. "Actually I'm hoping Brad will hang a little less with that group and more with me after we're married. He's expressed an interest in getting to know my friends."

"Really?" Amber sounded dubious. "Why?"

"Why? Because he loves me, of course. It's what couples do for each other."

Amber snorted. "Yeah right. I believe he loves you because you're lovable, but I'll reserve judgement on the he-wants-to-get-know-your-friends-thing."

They were halfway back to Portland when Cassie brought up the drapes. "Was Charlotte threatening Mavis with no raise or bonus?" she asked Amber. "Did I interpret that right?"

"She did more than that," Amber replied. "Your future mother-in-law offered Ms. Franks a fifty thousand dollar bribe to get her the event hall she wanted. The club will end up paying the full price on the drapes and the fifty thousand will go directly into the club manager's pocket."

"That's . . . awful." Cassie shuddered. "And dishonest, isn't it?"

Amber shrugged. "Nah, it's just business as usual in the uber rich circles."

CHAPTER 7

CASSIE SET her new lamp on the table next to her bed and stepped back to admire it. It looked exactly as she'd pictured it. The graceful twisted wrought iron base topped with a square, stained glass shade done in blues and greens with a soft gold accent, looked right at home next to her antique double-bow cherry bed.

She wiped the shade down with the damp cloth she held and sighed with pleasure. She had found the lamp in the second shop they tried, a place that had always intrigued her with its window display of eclectic vintage and funky new stock.

The young owner of the Treasure Chest had been pleasant as well as knowledgable. And he had asked Amber for a date as they were leaving, something that made Cassie happy. She suspected the main reason Amber had been acting so grumpy lately was because she had no one special in her life.

Cassie finished dusting the room and headed downstairs. Brad was tied up for the evening with one of the senior partners at his firm; a lawyer thing—she wasn't quite clear on the details—but thanks to the meeting with Mavis Franks she knew that Brad was hoping to make partner in the fall and suspected tonight's meeting might be to talk about that.

Cassie wandered her apartment. Sat and got up again. She felt at loose ends and restless. She didn't want to drive back into the city after being in Portland all day, but she didn't really want to sit around her apartment either. She decided to walk down to the estate's dock and grabbed a sweatshirt off its peg by the door.

Handsome scooted out the door in front of her. She welcomed his company. She knew that he would follow her most of the way to the small slice of waterfront that still belonged to the estate and then sit and wait for her to return. She didn't know why he wouldn't follow her all the way to the beach—some bad memory perhaps from the time before she found him?

The day's light was beginning to soften into dusk. The shadows beneath the great oaks and maples that graced the estate grounds deepened. Cassie made her way along the worn path, a well used dirt track beaten out of the grass from years of passing feet.

The short dock that ended in a small floating platform came into view, its rough boards weathered to a pale silver-gray. Cassie's steps sounded hollow as she followed the dock to the ramp that rolled back and forth on the platform with the rise and fall of the tide, connecting dock to platform.

Tonight the tide was near full and the ramp almost horizontal. Cassie stepped onto the platform and sat on the end of the ramp.

Waves slapped against the large, hollow fifty gallon metal drums that provided flotation to the platform. She watched them lap at the rocks bracketing the small crescent beach, now a mere sliver of silver sand. The gulls that filled the sky with motion and noise during the day had roosted, leaving a peaceful silence behind.

Cassie put her hands in her sweatshirt pockets and leaned back against the upright that supported the ramp's rail. Stars began to pop out in the deepening canopy overhead. To her right the lights of Portland twinkled along the curve of the bay.

She breathed in brine and tar, seaweed and a faint fishy odor. And salt, always the tang of fresh salt air.

The restlessness eased from Cassie's body. She loved the ocean. Had promised herself that she would always live within easy reach of its healing powers after she'd left her father's home. After nearly ten years of working up and down the eastern seaboard learning her trade she had returned to her roots.

Finding the apartment on the Rousch estate had been a stroke of luck. Since the family could no longer afford the upkeep on a boat, they had sold their Boston Whaler and rarely ventured down to their dock anymore. Most days it felt as if it and the small private beach belonged solely to her.

Cassie wondered what it would be like once she and Brad married and she moved into his family home. She would miss being able to walk to the water whenever she felt like it.

The Farland home was on the high side of Route 88, away from the water. Away from the blunt fury of storms, Brad had explained when she asked him why Brad Farland the First had chosen not to build next to the water.

Ah well. By the time September rolled around she should be used to the Farland house. She could always get her fix of ionized salt air at the boatyard as she intended to keep working after the wedding.

Cassie sat until the last rays of orange faded from the horizon and the June air turned too cool to sit out without a warmer jacket.

Handsome bumped her shin with his head when she met up with him on the path. He purred contentedly when she picked him up and carried him back to the apartment.

Cassie was almost at her door when she realized there was an extra shadow in the corner of the hallway. She stopped short. A chill of fear ran up her back. She took a step backwards, tensed her muscles to run.

Before she could turn to run away the shadow detached itself from the wall opposite her door and stepped into the light.

Pauli, dressed in faded jeans that hugged his hips and thighs and a worn chambray shirt with it's sleeves rolled up—exposing his well-muscled forearms—grinned at her. His blue eyes glinted with amusement.

"I wondered if you might be spending the night at Brad's," he said. "I was going to wait another fifteen and call it quits."

Relief followed by trepidation flowed through Cassie. Why was Pauli waiting for her? She wasn't sure she wanted to know, but of course she had to ask.

"What are you doing here?"

Pauli ignored her question. "Nice cat. What's his name? Were you taking him for a walk?"

Cassie set Handsome down and dug her keys out of her jean's front pocket. "His name is Handsome. I found him abandoned at the boatyard last year. He likes to go outside with me but he won't go near the water. He waits for me on the path."

Shut up, Cassie, you're babbling. A sure sign of nerves.

Handsome approached Pauli cautiously, then, apparently deciding he was okay, ribboned through Pauli's legs.

"Aren't you going to invite me in?" Pauli leaned down and plucked Handsome off the floor. His large, well-shaped hands stroked the cat's back. Handsome arched against the stroke and purred loudly, obviously enjoying it.

Traitor cat.

"Why are you here?" Cassie repeated, opening her door.

"I came to see you, of course." Pauli set Handsome on the floor and stepped into the apartment before Cassie could block him out.

Cassie rolled her eyes at him as she kicked off her sneakers. "Yeah, I get that, but why? *Why* are you here to see me?"

"Nice place." Pauli looked around the apartment, then began to drift through the room looking at Cassie's things. He liked what he saw. The place was colorful and comfortable. Exotic and interesting. Much like its owner.

An obviously old-fashioned, over-stuffed sofa covered with colorful Indian print throws dominated the right center of the room. More colorful prints covered the group of pillows tossed on he couch. Bright braided rugs covered patches of the wide-planked pine floor.

The windows were filled with green plants. Posters from the Maine state Common Ground Fair were framed in gray barn board and hung around the room. He walked over to inspect the one from 1990. The smiling pig made him smile back.

Books were strewn everywhere, piled on bookshelves and covering table tops and chairs.

He scanned the titles and saw a mix of fiction and non-fiction covering a wide variety of subjects. Interesting.

He spied the kitchen and headed for the refrigerator. He knew it was rude to invite himself in but he had been determined to see Cassie tonight. And he had not enjoyed standing in her dark hallway imagining her spending the night with Brad Farland.

Fiancé or no fiancé, Pauli didn't like thinking of Cassie with a man who played games. She was sweet and innocent, not wise to the ways of the assholes in the world.

It didn't matter that Pauli had never met Brad Farland. He knew the type—high-priced litigation lawyer always looking for the angle to get the better of others.

He'd discreetly asked around about Brad and learned that Brad was a player. A big player with big plans. Brad was laying the groundwork for a move into politics. In Maine the Farland name was synonymous with power. It wasn't healthy when one half of a couple held all the power.

Cassie had no family. Nobody to look out for her best interests. Despite his aversion to becoming involved, Pauli didn't want to see Cassie get hurt. There was something about her that drew him. Her complete lack of guile and the way she tried to look after people, even strangers.

"Do you keep anything to drink in here?" he asked as he opened the fridge door.

Cassie stood on the opposite side of the island that separated the kitchen alcove from the main room with her hands on her hips. "Make yourself at home, why don't you?"

Pauli turned his killer smile on her. "Thanks, I will. Can I pour you a glass of wine? I'd like one myself."

Cassie gave up. It was obvious that Pauli wouldn't leave until he accomplished whatever he'd come there for. She was surprised to realize that she felt glad for his company.

"Sure. I'd love a glass of wine. Glasses are in the upper cabinet to the left of the fridge."

While Pauli poured two glasses of wine she walked back to the door and removed her sweatshirt, hung it back on its peg, and tossed her keys in the wooden bowl she kept by the door.

She stepped to the compact disk player and cued up some old Paul Simon. African-inspired music flowed quietly from the speakers.

"Cheers," Pauli said as he handed her a glass and clinked his against it.

"Cheers. Now that you've made yourself at

home, care to tell me why you're here?" Her eyes narrowed. "And how did you know where I lived?"

Pauli walked over to her shelves of compact disks and flipped through them. She had an eclectic and widely varied collection of music; from classical to Gilbert and Sullivan to rock and roll to jazz and blues and modern artists. He approved. Music was important.

He turned away from the shelves and took a sip of wine, watching her over the rim of his glass. She stood leaning against the granite topped island, dressed in faded old jeans and a much-washed white tee shirt that was so thin he could see the outline of her nipples through it.

Cassie saw where he was looking. Her face heated and she knew she was blushing. "Oh for crying out loud. Men. You're all perverts." She pushed away from the island, crossed the room and grabbed her sweatshirt, pulling it back on before she faced him.

"Again. Why are you here and how did you find me?"

Pauli smirked at her. He couldn't help himself. Cassie was just so . . . cuddly looking was the term that sprang to mind. Her chestnut colored curls bouncing around her shoulders and her petite but curvaceous body made him want to wrap his arms around her and hold her close. Very, very close.

He did a mental head shake. Tonight was not the time. He was here for a different reason.

"I asked Stan where you lived," Pauli said. "He told me about helping you move your couch a few months ago. Nice couch by the way. It looks comfortable and inviting."

He moved away from the music shelves and sat on one end of the comfortable couch and patted the other cushion. "Have a seat, Cassie. I promise I won't bite. Or anything else. Not tonight anyway."

He smiled at her. He knew his smile held great power, the power to make women want to give him whatever he asked.

Fortunately Pauli had a strong code of ethics. All his siblings had been raised with a solid sense of right and wrong. Taking advantage of mere mortals fell under wrong. He never asked for anything a woman didn't already want to willingly give.

He could wait until Cassie wanted him the way he wanted her. The thought took him by surprise. He blinked. For a moment he forgot why he had come to see her.

Cassie moved to the couch, her eyes narrowed with suspicion. She sat on the far end and drew her legs up beneath her, sipped her wine. And waited for Pauli to tell her why he had invaded her space.

He looks at home here, she thought as she observed him.

Pauli looked relaxed, slouched against the couch pillows, wine glass resting on his flat stomach, fingers loose around the stem. His stockinged feet were stacked on her coffee table.

She hadn't even noticed when he'd taken off his boots. The fact that he had touched her.

Handsome leaped onto the couch and settled against Cassie's hips. Apparently he had no issues with Pauli invading their domain. He hissed at strangers and had stayed hidden while Stan drank a beer after helping her with the couch.

He wouldn't go near Brad and hid upstairs in the loft whenever Brad came to pick her up.

She thought of how the cat had ribboned between Pauli's legs in the hallway and relaxed slightly. Animals knew who to trust.

"So. You remember that group of people I ferried in at the end of the day yesterday?" Pauli asked. "You finished the job on the *Sea Maid* and rode in with them. The new dodger looks great, by the way. I heard Jerry Fowler say the same thing. He's really happy."

Cassie's fingers tightened on the stem of her wine glass. She suddenly had a bad feeling that she knew where this conversation was headed but she didn't know how to head it off.

"That's great. I'm glad Mr. Fowler's happy. He was a pleasure to work for. Some of the customers can be difficult."

Pauli nodded, kept his eyes on his glass. "Yeah. I get that. Do you remember the blonde? The one who was flirting with me? The one you warned to be careful on her way home?" He turned his head and his eyes bored into hers. "Do you remember warning her to be careful?"

Of course she remembered. Cassie always remembered. Every vision she'd ever had. Every unheeded warning. She couldn't rid herself of them. They stayed with her and haunted her, every single one of her failed attempts to help someone avoid injury or heartache.

Cassie couldn't speak. Her throat felt constricted, as if a fist had taken hold of her neck and squeezed. She jerked her head, a small movement.

"Well, what I was wondering, Cassie," Brad went on, still watching her, "is why you warned the blonde. What did you see that made you do that? Because she's definitely one of the difficult ones and I just don't see you making a point of speaking with her unless you felt you had a good reason."

Cassie ran her fingers up and down the stem of her glass. What could she tell him? That she'd been having visions since she was a young teen? That they always came true? That no one ever believed her?

She swallowed, trying to ease the tightness in her throat.

"I, uh, I had a feeling that the woman was going to get hurt driving home." She shrugged, tried to affect an air of nonchalance. "Intuition, maybe. I only told her to be careful, that's all. Why do you ask?"

"Did you see the news last night?"

"No. I read and went to bed." Liar! She hoped Pauli couldn't read the lie in her eyes. If he could, he ignored it.

"The blonde, whose name is Melody Harbush by the way, was in a car accident on her way home from the marina and had to be taken to the hospital by ambulance. Apparently she was in a hurry to get home. According to witnesses, she tried to pass the car in front of her on a curve. She met a car coming from the opposite direction and bailed out in the ditch. Rolled her car three times."

Cassie's left hand began to tremble. She tucked it under her thigh to keep it still. "That's terrible. Do you know how badly she was hurt?"

"Facial contusions, concussion. She was lucky. There were no boulders in the ditch. She suffered no broken bones or internal injuries. Her Beemer was loaded with air bags and they all deployed."

Pauli waited but Cassie said nothing else. He knew there was more that Cassie wasn't telling him but he wasn't sure how to pull it out of her. Time to change the subject, he decided.

"Have you had dinner?" he asked.

Relieved that he wasn't going to push on Melody Harbush, Cassie shook her head. "No. I made some really good chicken and rice soup and pumpernickel bread. I can heat it up if you'd like."

Pauli smiled at her. "Sounds great. I can't remember the last time I had homemade soup."

He followed Cassie into the kitchen and found what he needed to set the table while she heated the soup and bread, set out butter. While they ate they talked of other things.

Cassie was surprised and envious to learn that Pauli had lived all over the world and had a large family: two brothers and a sister, parents, aunts, uncles and numerous cousins. Even a new sister-in-law with a niece or nephew on the way.

After dinner Pauli helped her do the dishes. She walked him to the door when he was ready to leave.

"Thanks for the wine and dinner," he said, looking down at her. Before she could answer he cupped her chin in his palm and leaned down to kiss her.

She tasted sweet, a mix of the homemade chocolate chip cookies they'd had for dessert and the wine, and something elusive that could only be essence of Cassandra.

At his first touch Cassie froze with shock. Then her lips softened and she leaned into the kiss. Pauli was a superb kisser. Her lips tingled and her heart thumped in her chest.

He broke the kiss off and rubbed his thumb lightly over her lips. "See you at the boatyard on Monday."

He was gone before Cassie could say anything. She stood half in shock, her heart still hammering from the unexpected intensity of Pauli's touch.

She touched her finger to her still tingling lips. Oh my. She had never experienced a kiss like that.

And then it struck her. She had *kissed* Pauli back. She had *responded* to his touch. She was engaged to Brad and she had kissed Pauli back. She had leaned into him, had participated fully. What sort of skank-woman was she anyhow?

One who would never let that happen again, she decided, and shut and locked her door.

CHAPTER 8

LATE MONDAY MORNING Cassie looked up from her sewing machine to see a family of four standing uncertainly at the sail loft door. She looked around the space for Jonathan who usually dealt with loft visitors but he was nowhere in sight.

Cassie climbed out of her recessed box and slid across the sail loft floor in her thick socks.

"Hi! Jonathan isn't here at the moment. Is there anything I can help you with? I'm Cassie," she said as she held her hand out to the mother.

The couple smiled at her and both shook her hand.

"We're here to pick up a set of cushions for

our boat," answered the man. "The name is Mac-Dougal. Sam MacDougal."

"I just finished them Friday," Cassie said with a smile. "I understand it was a rush job. You're taking a trip up the coast with the whole family, right?"

"Yeah. We're going all the way to Canada!" said the boy, his eyes shining. "We'll be gone three whole weeks!"

Cassie judged the boy's age to be around ten. Brown-eyed, freckled, and with an endearing cowlick in his short brown hair, she thought he looked like a handful. Just like a young boy should look. Mischievous and full of fun.

She looked at the sister and frowned inwardly. The girl—who looked to be a couple years older than her brother—looked unnaturally pale under her tan. Was she not a sailor? Afraid to go on such a long trip?

"I'll get those cushions for you," Cassie said. "If you wouldn't mind waiting here it'll only take me a minute. We don't allow shoes on the loft floor."

"Cool! You get to work in your socks! I bet it's fun to slide on this huge floor." The boy looked as if he was about to take off his shoes and try it out.

"You do as Cassie asked and wait right here,

Joshua," his mother said, clamping a firm hand on the boy's shoulder.

Cassie grinned and retrieved the cushions. While she filled out the paperwork she watched the daughter. Something was definitely wrong there. Could just be fear. Not everyone took to boating.

She helped the family carry the long cushions out to the flatbed dolly they had already loaded with supplies for their trip. As she was securing the cushions she was struck with a sudden image of the girl lying in her bunk, sweating and puking. Not seasick. Deathly ill.

She grabbed the mother's arm and pulled her aside. "Mrs. MacDougal, I know I've only just met you, but your daughter looks ill to me. Perhaps you should have her checked out before you head to where there's no easily available medical care."

The mother looked at her daughter and frowned. "She does look a little pale. I'll call my brother. He's a doctor and can probably squeeze her in for a quick look. A couple hours delay won't hurt us. Thank you for pointing it out."

Cassie left them and went back to work feeling a little unsettled. This was the first time anybody had paid attention and acted upon one of her warnings. The usual reaction was words and/or looks of disbelief.

She shook her head and put it away. She had plenty to keep her mind occupied.

Just as she was gathering her things and preparing to punch out at the end of the day, Jonathan took a call.

"Cassie, wait." He beckoned her to the phone. "Call for you."

Cassie took her shoes back off and padded over to Jonathan's counter. "Hello? This is Cassie."

"Cassie? This is Myra MacDougal. I wanted to thank you for this morning. I took Sarah to my brother and he had her admitted to the hospital right away. She had an emergency appendectomy. If you hadn't pointed out how pale she was I shudder to think what would have happened. Bruce, my brother, said Sarah's appendix would have burst. She could have died before we got help for her."

Cassie heard the tears in Myra MacDougal's voice. "I'm so glad I said something, Mrs. Mac-Dougal. Will Sarah be okay now?"

"Yes. She came through the operation just fine. We have to reschedule our trip of course, but that's nothing. I don't know how Sam and I could've survived losing our little girl that way.

Thank you. Thank you. Thank you. If there's ever anything we can do for you you have only to ask."

"Knowing that Sarah will be fine is thanks enough, Mrs. MacDougal. I appreciate the call. I would have worried about Sarah."

Cassie hung up. Feeling a little dazed, she put her shoes back on and drove home. Her visions always came true. Over the years she had come to understand and expect that.

This was the first time since she'd started experiencing the visions that her warning had *prevented* the vision from coming true. The first time a vision felt as if maybe it had a higher purpose—that maybe *she* had a higher purpose. Maybe she could be more than just a psychic freak.

She prayed this was the start of a new trend.

Cassie managed to avoid Pauli for the remainder of the week. Whenever she had to go out to a boat for a fitting or installation she timed it so that Pauli was either off duty or already out ferrying others and Amos was at the dock in the second launch.

It hadn't been easy. Twice she'd started for the dock and recognized Pauli at the helm and turned back. Both times she'd had to tell Jonathan that she'd forgotten something. A lie that made her boss think she was scatterbrained, or worse, incompetent.

She knew her actions were cowardly, and she also knew that by avoiding Pauli she was giving weight and importance to his kiss. Just because she'd had such a . . . *visceral* . . . reaction to it didn't mean that the kiss meant anything. It was just a kiss after all.

What it meant, she finally decided, was that Pauli was one hell of a kisser, a man who'd obviously had lots of practice, and *that's* what she had reacted to. It was to be expected that a man who looked like a gift from the gods would be an expert with women.

She refused to allow herself to think about what he could do to her in bed. Not going there. No way. Despite her effort to shut it out her toes curled slightly at the thought, brief as it was.

She was relieved when Friday night rolled around and she had a double date with Brad and one of his fellow lawyers and the lawyer's wife. She hadn't seen Brad since the meeting at his mother's club although he made a point to call her every night.

Cassie dressed carefully in cream-colored

linen slacks and a lightweight sage green sweater, fastened large gold hoops in her ears and slid a couple gold bangles onto her arm. She owned very little jewelry, but like her other possessions what she owned was good quality.

She eyed her reflection in the free-standing cheval mirror with approval. She looked like a woman who could be married to an up and coming lawyer. Understated and classy. The downstairs buzzer rang. Cassie told Handsome not to wait up for her and ran down to meet Brad.

"You look beautiful, sweetheart," Brad said as he kissed her lightly and held the door of his Mercedes for her.

Cassie slid into the leather seat and fastened the seatbelt. "Where are we eating tonight?"

"Warren's. It's a new place that Adam and Cherise wanted to try."

"Adam and Cherise? I haven't met them yet, have I?"

"No. I haven't met Cherise yet either, but Adam is okay. We're working several cases together. He's sharp and thorough."

Cassie waited until Brad pulled out of her drive onto Route 88. "We haven't seen each other all week. I was a little surprised you suggested a double date."

Brad glanced at her and grinned, the dimple in his right cheek deepening. "Are you saying you missed me? I like that. I've had to put in a lot of extra hours this week. The life of a junior member in a big firm. We do most of the grunt work while the big guns swoop in afterward and take all the glory.

"As for the double date, Adam's only been with the firm six months. They moved here from Minneapolis and from what he says I get the feeling that Cherise is suffering from culture shock. I thought it might be nice if you two could get to know each other, maybe become friends."

"Mmmmm." Cassie wasn't so sure she was what Cherise was looking for in a friend, especially when Brad told her that Cherise was also an attorney. In Cassie's admittedly limited experience, attorneys tended to have little interest in those not connected to the law.

Warren's turned out to have typical upscale-yuppie decor and a predictable menu. The dining area featured small, square tables clad in copper and placed close together, seating four with barely enough room for drinks let alone food dishes.

Green plants, predominantly ferns and pothos, hung from the ceiling. Mirrors interspersed with pictures of Portland landmarks from before the great fire of 1866 lined the walls. Cassie knew the mirrors were there to to give the illusion of space, but for her they didn't work.

Sound bounced off the hard surfaces and the room felt small and confining rather than intimate.

A long, copper-clad bar separated the dining area from the larger packed bar. The roomy bar was where management made it's money and where they had focused most of their efforts. A comfortable drinking customer stayed longer and spent more. From her days waitressing Cassie knew that unlike food, there was a significant mark-up on booze.

There were several seating areas in the bar featuring long, leather couches grouped with several deep, slouchy chairs and low tables. A central fireplace, open on four sides, anchored the space.

For the drinkers who arrived too late to snag a couch or chair, high top tables with deeply padded stools ran along the three walls of the bar.

The circular bar where the bartenders worked also sported padded swivel stools with backs and a sturdy brass foot rail for those who liked to stand.

Two well-built attractive bartenders, one male and one female, both dressed in snug tank tops and khaki shorts, worked steadily mixing drinks and pulling beer taps.

Fortunately the dining area was not as crowded as the bar or Cassie didn't think she'd have been able to eat. She settled on the Caesar salad with grilled shrimp and a glass of white wine.

She glanced at Brad who was deep in conversation with Adam about some big litigation case they were both involved with. Adam had turned out to be a darker clone of Brad. Handsome, obviously from money, he oozed an air of entitlement.

Cassie took an instant dislike to him. She turned her attention away from the men to Cherise, who looked exceedingly bored.

Cherise was the female version of the men and reminded Cassie of the blonde twit at Charlotte's club. She was also blonde, with classic features, tall and slim, with eau d'snoot wafting off her lovely gym-toned body.

"So," Cassie said, smiling brightly at the woman sitting catty-corner to her, "what do you think of Portland? Do you like living near the ocean? It has to be quite a change for you."

Cherise shrugged and took a sip of her vodka martini. "Frankly I can't understand the attraction. Living next to an ocean that's too cold to swim in seems a waste to me."

Cassie raised her eyebrows in surprise. "I thought Brad said you lived in Minneapolis. You have winter there, or am I wrong? You should be used to the cold."

Cherise's eyes tracked the male bartender. "What's that have to do with living next to the North Atlantic? If I'm going to be on the ocean I want one I can enjoy—like the Caribbean, or the south of France. Even Greece."

"Huh." Cassie cast around for another subject. "Tell me about your job. You work for a small firm on Exchange Street, right?"

Cherise's eyes cut to Cassie and hardened. "Are you saying I'm not good enough to get a place in a large firm?"

Shocked by the animosity, Cassie's mouth hung open for a few seconds. She wished Brad would stop talking to Adam and help her out. So far nothing she had said to Cherise was going over very well.

"No—I wasn't implying that at all," she finally

managed. "I happen to like the Old Port area. And actually I think it would be better working for a small firm because you wouldn't get lost in the crowd. Big fish, small pond theory. There are over one hundred attorneys at Brad's law firm. Too many for any one to stand out unless he or she makes partner."

Cherise went back to watching the bartender. "Shows what you know. The big firms are where the opportunities are."

Cassie decided not to pursue the topic. Maybe the reason Cherise reacted to her question the way she did was because she *wasn't* good enough to get into one of the large firms.

"I need another drink." Cherise ignored their waitress who was hovering nearby and headed for the bar, leaving her half-finished martini on the table.

Cassie watched as she smiled at the male bartender, then wrote something on a cocktail napkin and slipped it to him. He pocketed the napkin, handed her a fresh martini and winked before turning away.

Cherise came back to the table looking much happier.

Fortunately their food was served right after Cherise sat down. Cassie had no desire to make further conversation with the prickly female attorney and the food gave her an excuse to keep quiet.

Brad and Adam eventually returned their attention to the women and everyone made small talk while they ate. Cassie couldn't help but notice that Cherise smiled at the men—especially Brad—a lot, and pretty much ignored Cassie.

When Adam suggested they find a music club after their meal Cassie begged a headache and asked Brad to take her home. She let out a huge sigh when she settled into the dark quiet of Brad's Mercedes.

"Don't ever make me have dinner with that pair again," she said when they were on their way home.

Brad turned a surprised look on Cassie. "Why not? They're intelligent, interesting people. I thought Cherise was delightful."

Cassie made a face. "Sure. She was delightful to *you*. You're a rich, handsome lawyer. Every time I tried to start a conversation with her she practically snapped my head off. And I'll tell you something else—she cheats on Adam."

Brad's expression changed to shock, then became thoughtful. "Are you sure? Why would you say that?"

"I saw her give the hot bartender guy her phone number. I don't think it had anything to do with offering legal help."

"Mmmmm. Interesting. We'll have to invite them to the wedding reception of course, but I can probably avoid any more double dates with them if you really didn't enjoy yourself."

"Thank you. And I really didn't enjoy them." She hesitated a moment. "Why do we have to invite them to the reception?" she asked carefully.

"All of the senior attorneys in my firm will be invited," Brad answered. He passed a slow-moving, rusted out Subaru, pulled back into the travel lane. Moonlight sparkled off the bay waters to Cassie's right.

"I also have to invite any of the others that I've worked with. If I leave anyone out and they become someone important it could come back to bite me down the road. Better to avoid that," he continued.

Cassie shifted sideways on the seat so she was looking at Brad's profile. "I don't understand. Why would any of them care if they aren't invited? You invite the ones you work with the most and any you've developed a relationship with. The others should understand. Weddings are for family and friends."

Brad shook his head. "It's not that simple. Part of being an effective lawyer is currying favor with those in power."

"Ahhh. I thought the law was supposed to be spelled out so that it's fair to everyone."

Brad reached over and patted her hand. "In theory it is. But a good lawyer thinks of the future and keeps his thumb on the up and coming, as well as the ones whose power is on the wane."

"Did you learn this from your father?"

"Him. And Mother. She has a real knack for knowing how to play the game. She was a big help to Father. My great-grandfather, Brad Far-land the First, was governor of Maine for two terms."

"I know, your mother told me." Then it hit her. "Are you thinking of getting involved in politics, Brad?"

He lifted one shoulder in a half shrug. "I've been toying with the idea. With my family's record there are people who expect it of me and have already offered their support. My father would have run for the office if he hadn't died unexpectedly."

He turned to look at her, his eyes bright in the lights from the dash. "How would you feel about that? You could be the governor's wife one day."

Stunned, Cassie faced forward and turned her head to look out the side window. She tried to order her thoughts and feelings. Brad wanted to run for office? Not only that, he was aiming for the state's top position—governor! She turned back to him.

"Does your mother know?"

"She's the one who suggested I consider it."

"I see." But she didn't, not really. Why would Brad ask her to marry him and neglect to mention that he dreamed of becoming governor of the state of Maine?

Or was this a recent thing, something that had only come up in the last week or so? Brad had been working long hours and they hadn't had much time to talk. Something this big needed to be discussed in person, not over the phone.

"Believe it or not my mother was a lot like you when she married Father," Brad went on. "She was an average citizen, someone who knew what it means to live on a budget. But she was smart and worked hard. By the time Father had his heart attack and died she had carved a place at the top of Portland society for herself. You won't have to tread that path. Once we're married you'll be accepted as one of us. Mother's position guarantees that."

Cassie shook her head. She thought of the blonde at the club and the way she had looked down her nose at Cassie and Amber. It would take a lot more than Charlotte Farland's position in society to change that attitude. And the blonde wouldn't be the only one.

Oh, certainly the blonde and the others would pretend to accept Cassie. They wouldn't risk Charlotte's wrath. But deep down? She'd never be one of them.

"I don't know, Brad. When Amber and I met you at your mother's club last weekend I realized how different I am from the members there. We have different. . . values."

"Nonsense. You'll see. You have more in common with them than you realize."

To Brad that was a compliment. To Cassie it sounded more like a put down. She shuddered inwardly.

"What about my friends?" she asked. "Where will they fit?"

Brad pulled into Cassie's drive and parked next to the door leading up to her apartment. He shut off the engine and took her hand in his.

"Why don't you plan a dinner for your co-workers on Wednesday night next week? I'll make sure I get it off. We'll have it at my place, then you won't have to do any extra work. My cook will take care of everything."

Cassie thought of Stan and Amber sitting around Brad's formal dining table and frowned. They'd be uncomfortable. Heck, *she'd* be uncomfortable.

"I'm glad you want to spend time with my friends, but I'd rather have dinner here. I like to cook, Brad, and I think they'll be more comfortable at my place—at least until they get to know you better."

Brad leaned across and kissed her lightly. "Great. If that makes you happy it's a plan. I'll have to work late every night to justify taking that Wednesday night off so I won't see you before then, but I'll call. Should we plan on dinner at seven?"

Cassie thought of her working friends, people whose day started at dawn, people who typically ate their dinners between five and six. They'd starve if they had to wait until seven to eat!

"Let's make it six-thirty. My friends all have early starts to their work day and they'll want to eat and get home to bed." She'd just have to serve snacks and drinks to hold them until the meal.

"Six-thirty then. Goodnight, Cassie. I'll call tomorrow." Brad kissed her lightly.

Cassie walked to the door that led up to her apartment and let herself in. Her head was whirling. Governor's wife? That bomb had fallen right out of the blue. Brad had never even hinted at an interest in politics before tonight.

Could a poor girl from Gorham's Corner rise that high? It seemed impossible, but then so had the dream that someone like Brad—handsome, upper class Brad—would ever want to marry a nobody like Cassandra Brown.

She supposed that she could learn how to be a governor's wife in the same way she'd learned how to design and build canvas—with hard work and dedication. She would make mistakes for sure, but hopefully nothing that would reflect badly on Brad.

She pushed the thoughts away. There was no point in worrying about something that may never happen. She needed to concentrate on learning how to be a good lawyer's wife, or at least as good as she was capable of.

Brad was definitely wrong about one thing. She was *nothing* like Charlotte Farland. Nor would she ever be.

CHAPTER 9

CASSIE CIRCLED her dining table and frowned. She needed more chairs. Everyone but Pauli was bringing a spouse, or, in the case of Amber, her new boyfriend. Including Brad and herself, that made eleven diners and only six chairs.

She grabbed her phone and made a couple quick calls. Checking her wall clock, a large grinning cat with a swinging tail, she sprinted for the shower when she saw how late it was. She had gotten caught up in arranging plates of cheese and sliced fruit and crackers and forgotten about the time.

Fortunately dinner was in the oven. She had assembled the large lasagna the previous evening and prepped two loaves of garlic bread. They lay wrapped in foil, waiting to join the lasagna to heat through. She had taken the easy way out and purchased bagged salad, something she hated to do, but made her own dressing to compensate. Food was done.

She took a fast shower and dressed in comfortable jeans and a tee. Took a couple passes through the great room plumping pillows and smoothing the couch throws. She loaded the CD player with easy dinner music, took a last look around, and wiped her damp palms on her pants.

Why was she so nervous? She knew and liked these people. She didn't know the three wives very well, but she had met them several times and got along fine with them. Of course her vision had told her that Doreen would leave Stan soon, but she could push that out of her head for the evening. And she had met Amber's date Tyler at his store and liked him instantly.

Pauli would be the only unattached guest. Cassie had told him he could bring someone but he had declined.

She would rather he brought a date. Pauli coming alone made her think of the last time he stood in this room. When he had kissed her and left her dazzled.

· · ·

"Hey Mrs. Haskell, let me carry that chair for you." Pauli reached forward and easily plucked the chair from Kathryn Haskell's hands. She gave him a warm smile and a relieved "thank you."

Pauli liked Cassie's boss's wife. Kathryn always had a friendly word for him whenever she came to the marina. More important, she seemed to be happily married to Jonathan and never tried to flirt with Pauli. He found that refreshing and liked her all the more for it.

They were crossing the parking pad next to the estate's carriage house/garage, headed to the stairwell that led to Cassie's apartment. Behind them, Stan and his wife Doreen roared up in Stan's big Ford pick-up. Stan needed the roomy cab to hold his bulk. Next to him Doreen looked like a twig compared to Stan's redwood mass.

"Thanks, Pauli." Jonathan grinned at him. "I tried carrying two at once but stumbled and nearly fell. I think I may buy Cassie a chair for Christmas this year. Seems silly to invite more guests than you can seat, but that's typical Cassie."

Pauli didn't get a chance to find out what Jonathan meant by that because Amos, the other launch driver, honked his horn as he and his wife Sandra pulled in.

Stan grabbed two chairs from the bed of his truck and joined the group gathering at the base of the stairs. "We must be dining at Cassie's," he said. "I don't know anyone else who would call at the last minute and ask us to bring our own chair." He grinned. "I like it."

Pauli saw the redhead who worked in the sail loft with Cassie arrive with a slim, dark, pony-tailed man. They smiled and waved and the driver grabbed a colorfully painted chair from the back seat.

"Looks like the chair brigade has arrived," he said as they joined the group. "I'm Tyler." Introductions were made all around with much laughter as they shifted their burdens to shake hands.

Before they could start up the stairs a Mercedes drove in.

"That must be the fiancé," Amos whispered. "I hear he's loaded."

"Maybe he'll spring for some new chairs for Cassie." Amos's wife Sandra winked at Kathryn. "What good is having money if you don't spend it on the person you love, right?" The two women grinned at each other.

Brad exited the Mercedes and strode over to the group. He looked immaculate and over-dressed in crisp chinos and designer polo shirt, especially compared to the worn jeans and tee shirts of the other guests.

"You must be Cassie's friends. I'm Brad Farland III." He frowned at the chair in Tyler's hands. "What's with all the chairs? Is this some gag?"

Amber led the way up the stairs. "Nope," she said over her shoulder. "There are eleven of us dining and Cassie only has six chairs. So some of us brought our own."

Brad frowned. "That's ridiculous. I told Cassie we could have this dinner at my place. I can easily seat twenty at my dining table and I have a chef."

"Of course you do," muttered Amber, but Pauli knew that Brad hadn't heard her. Just as well, he thought. He guessed that this dinner was important to Cassie and she would want everyone to get along.

They filed into her apartment, laughing and jostling with the chairs while they removed their shoes. All except Brad, who carefully wiped his leather loafers on the rug.

Cassie's guests ate, drank, laughed, and talked for the next two and a half hours. The lasagna drew compliments from everyone. Only yummy noises were heard while they savored the warm blueberry cake with vanilla ice cream that followed.

Katherine Haskell pushed away from the table and sipped her coffee. "That was an amazing meal, Cassie. You are truly an exceptional cook. It's a good thing I'm not married to you or I'd weigh three hundred pounds. You'd better be careful, Brad. Too much of Cassie's good cooking and you'll lose that fine figure."

Brad smiled at Kathryn. "That won't be a problem. I have a chef who is trained to create nutritional, healthy meals. And once we move to the governor's mansion we'll have a staff to deal with meals."

Cassie's gaze flew to Brad's face. She had first heard of his political ambitions only a few days before. At the time Brad made it sound as if it was a future possibility. Tonight he made it sound as if running for governor was a certainty.

Only Pauli caught the distress in Cassie's eyes before she lowered her gaze. For a moment no one spoke.

"You're planning to run for governor?" Jonathan asked. "What does that entail?"

Brad stretched his legs in front of him and settled back in his chair. "Well, lots of money for starters. And more voters than my opponent. After that the two most common routes are either success in a Maine-based business or success as a lawyer. Fortunately I work for the largest law firm in the state and I've recently been told that I'll be made partner in the fall. I'll have the full support of the firm behind me."

"Brad!" Cassie said, surprised. "You didn't tell me that. That's wonderful news. I know you've worked hard for a partnership."

"I didn't get a chance to tell you. Carson only told me this afternoon."

Cassie felt a small twinge of disappointment that Brad hadn't called her immediately to share his news with her privately but she set it aside. Of course he was excited and wanted to share with others. Partnership was a big deal in the legal world.

Brad turned his attention back to Jonathan. "While being partner is an honor in its own right, being partner in a big, prestigious firm will give me clout and raise my visibility to the voters. And that's the tricky part. The people have to feel that they know me well enough to vote for me. I'm figuring I'll run in four years, the election cycle after this fall's."

Amber helped Cassie pile empty plates and

carry them into the kitchen. "Did you know Brad was planning to run for governor when he asked you to marry him?" she whispered as she scraped the few scraps into the trash.

Cassie shook her head. "No, I didn't. He told me last weekend that he was thinking about it. Tonight's the first I've heard that it's a definite plan."

She filled the right hand sink with hot, soapy water and slid a stack of plates in. She wished Brad hadn't announced his goal of governorship to her friends before she'd had a chance to discuss it with him in private.

"Well, Mrs. Governor. That's an ambitious man you're engaged to. I wish him luck," Kathryn said as she entered the kitchen alcove with more dishes.

"I like it," Sandra said as she crowded in and set her load of wine glasses on the counter. "It will be good to know people in high places. You never know when you'll need them." She grinned at Cassie. "You'll be my new best friend."

Cassie laughed. She knew Sandra was only joking and she appreciated the way Sandra had lightened the tone of the conversation.

She insisted the women leave the dishes for

her to do later but they refused. Many hands made light work and twenty minutes later the last guest was leaving—with their chairs.

All except Tyler, who insisted his was a gift and a thank you for her wonderful meal. Cassie hugged him and waggled her eyebrows at Amber behind his back. Tyler was a genuinely nice guy and she was happy for her friend.

Brad was the last to leave. At the door he took both her hands in his. "That went well, I think," he said. "It was a good opportunity to see how others live and find out what issues are important to them. I'll be able to use that in my campaign."

"They're my friends, Brad, not subjects to be polled. Is that why you suggested this dinner?"

Brad had the grace to look a little sheepish. "I thought you understood that. Your friends aren't the kind of people I usually socialize with, Cass. Jonathan's okay. He's a shrewd businessman and I appreciate that. Pauli puzzles me. He's lived all over the world. He understands the layers of society. He obviously comes from money. I'm surprised he's satisfied working a summer job as a lowly launch driver."

Cassie pulled her hands away from Brad's. "I'm sorry my friends don't measure up to your standards," she said stiffly. "And I have to wonder why you want to marry me. *I'm* only a lowly canvas worker. I have no money and no connections."

Brad wrapped his arms around her, drew her in. "You have an inner beauty that rises above your circumstances," he said into her hair. "And I'm smart enough to recognize it."

Partially mollified, Cassie relaxed against him. "Would you like to spend the night?" She felt Brad kiss the top of her head before he dropped his arms and stepped back.

"No can do. I made you a promise that we'd wait until our wedding night and now you know why."

Cassie wrinkled her brow. "You did?" She couldn't remember any such promise. "Why?"

"Because when I announce that I'm running for office and the press starts digging into our private lives I don't want there to be anything there for them to find. You will remain above reproach and I will be seen as a man who can control his baser urges." He laid a light kiss on Cassie's mouth and left.

She stood by the door for several minutes, unable to move. They weren't having sex because Brad wanted to impress the press? Holy mother of god. All this time she had thought that he was holding back out of respect for her.

And now she had a new worry. When the press started digging into her life would they learn about her visions?

CHAPTER 10

PAULI SPIED Cassie standing on the dock with her tool bag and several bags of canvas. He gunned the launch motor just a little, but enough to beat Amos to the dock.

He saw Cassie's eyes dart out toward Amos's launch and smiled to himself. He knew she'd been avoiding him. Two weeks had passed since her dinner party. Three since he'd kissed her.

He could still feel the hum in his body. A hum that made Pauli want more.

He wasn't going to let Cassie avoid him any longer. Today he had outmaneuvered her. A wide grin split his face as he neared the gas dock. He was going to get to the bottom of Cassandra Brown, no matter what it took.

Cassie was hiding something, something big. Pauli had a touch of *the sight* himself, and he was pretty sure it ran strong in Cassie. He didn't understand why she felt compelled to lie about it. Honesty was important to Pauli. He held it right up there with music, for which he had a grand passion.

"Morning, Cassie," he said, keeping his tone mild as the launch bumped against the dock. Avoiding eye contact, Cassie took the bow line and made it fast.

"Hand me your tool bag." Pauli reached out a hand. "Looks like you have a big installation today. That's twice the amount of canvas you usually carry."

Cassie hesitated.

He could see the resignation in her eyes when she realized that waiting for Amos to reach the dock would make it obvious that she was avoiding Pauli. Still not looking at him, she handed him her heavy tool bag followed by the two long canvas bags.

"Where are we headed this morning?" Pauli grinned again. He couldn't help it, he was enjoying himself.

Cassie climbed into the launch and sat amidships instead of in the stern like she usually did.

"Thomas Porter, mooring one ninety-two. The *Family Man.*"

"Roger that." Pauli focused his attention on driving the launch and waited for Cassie to relax. He could see that her shoulders were stiff and tense under the lightweight cotton shirt she wore, and she held her hands clenched together between her tanned knees. He couldn't help but notice that they were very pretty tanned knees.

"Your lasagna was great, by the way," he said aloud. "I don't know if I stopped eating long enough to tell you that. Thanks for inviting me. I know without a date I made the table numbers odd. My mother would have invited a single female friend to even them up. I appreciate that you didn't."

Cassie's gaze flitted to Pauli's face and away again. "Oh. Huh. I never even considered that. Not that it would have made a difference. Amber is the only single female I know well enough to invite for dinner and she had a date."

Pauli took it as a good sign that he had Cassie talking. He pressed on. "Amber's boyfriend is Tyler, right? I liked him. He didn't put on airs and he was interesting. I'm going to check out his shop, see if I can find something unusual to send my folks."

Cassie smiled and relaxed a little. Maybe Pauli wasn't going to ask difficult questions about Melody Harbush's accident after all.

"Yeah, I like Tyler too. His shop is great. I bought a lamp for the table beside my bed from him the day Amber met him. It's exactly what I was looking for: well-made and a blend of arty and utilitarian. Tyler has an eye for that kind of thing."

Pauli smiled at her as he guided the launch expertly between two sleek sailboats. "I'm guessing the chair he gifted you came from his shop?"

Cassie nodded. "Yes. It was a nice gift. Generous and unexpected. A little like Tyler himself. There's the *Family Man*," she said pointing.

Pauli veered between two large sport-fishing vessels and approached the older *Family Man*. He whistled in appreciation when he pulled up next to her wooden hull and saw all the oiled teak and brightwork.

"Wow. This is a beauty," he said, grabbing the rail and tying the launch.

Cassie scrambled onto the wooden deck and reached for her bags as Pauli handed them to her. "Mr. Porter has great taste in boats," she agreed. "I think this is one of the prettiest boats I've had the pleasure to work on. Probably because it's older and has style. Forty-two foot with a twenty-foot beam, so it's very stable for what he does, which is motor around the islands with his kids and grandchildren. It has four sleep cabins, a galley, and a large salon below."

"What did you design for Mr. Porter?" Pauli asked as he handed her the last bag.

"He wants to be able to close off the open extension behind the wheelhouse so the family can sit with him in inclement weather," Cassie answered. "Thanks for the lift."

But Pauli wasn't ready to leave yet. He'd finally gotten Cassie talking and he was nowhere near ready to end the conversation.

"What color canvas did he go with? I hope you talked him into something other than the boring but-very-nautical bright blue that ninety percent of the boats in the marina use."

Now Cassie grinned. "I did. I convinced him that a deep green would look very upscale and classy, especially with all the teak. And I talked him into zip-out windows with screens so the family can sit on deck in the evenings and not be driven inside by the bugs."

"Good for you. How long will it take to install all that?"

"I figure I'll need most of the day."

He could see that she was anxious to get started. Inspiration hit him as he grabbed the line holding the two boats together. "I'll be back with a couple of Italian sandwiches around midday. What do want to drink?"

Pauli untied the line and let the launch drift away from the *Family Man.*

Panic flared in Cassie. "That's not necessary, Pauli. I'll be fine," she called out. "I have granola bars." But it was too late. Pauli had turned his back and was motoring away.

"Dammit." She didn't want to eat lunch with Pauli.

No, that was only partly true. She *wanted* to share lunch with Pauli, she enjoyed his company. And because she enjoyed his company, she *didn't* want to have lunch with him.

Sometimes she really confused herself.

True to his word, Pauli showed up at midday. He tied off the launch, turned up the radio so he wouldn't miss any calls, and leaped nimbly onto the *Family Man's* deck.

"Do you mind if I look around before we eat? It's really a lovely craft."

Cassie waved a hand. "Go ahead. I want to get these last three fasteners into this curtain before I break to eat anyway."

She had spent the morning lecturing herself until she had eventually settled into a resigned fugue over eating lunch with the incredibly attractive Pauli.

Eating lunch didn't mean she had to kiss him. Eating lunch wasn't cheating on Brad. She and Pauli were co-workers after all. It made sense for them to spend time together.

So why did she feel so guilty about it? She watched the very fine view of Pauli's backside disappear below. Her pulse quickened.

"And *that's* why this is a bad idea," she muttered to herself.

When Pauli returned to the deck Cassie was ready for him, determined to keep things light and impersonal. "Let's eat. I'm famished!"

Pauli settled with his back against the stern and handed Cassie a white-wrapped package. "A whole Italian for each of us. No onions, extra black olives on yours." He squinted at Cassie. "A disservice to the inventor of the Italian, I must point out."

He handed Cassie a bag of salt and vinegar potato chips and an unsweetened ice tea.

"How did you know I drink ice tea?" she asked, taking a welcome swig from the bottle. The cold liquid slid down her throat and refreshed her. She wasted no time unwrapping her sandwich and took a large, unladylike bite.

"Stan. Since you neglected to tell me what you drink I told him to get your usual. He picked this up for me since I couldn't get away." He could have gotten away, but the time to run to the sandwich place would've eaten into his lunch hour and therefore the time he had to spend with Cassie.

They ate in a companionable silence until not even a potato chip crumb remained. The marina and bay were in full swing. It looked to Cassie as if half the city had chosen this week to take vacation time to enjoy Maine's short season of warm.

The open water beyond the *Family Man* was bustling with boats of every size and type. Cassie picked out the yellow, green, and blue spinnaker that Amber had sewn up a few weeks before and made a note to tell her friend how great it looked filled with air, billowing off the front of a racing sailboat.

Laughter and shouts mingled with the cry of seabirds and the clang of metal shrouds and stays from moored sailboats. The *Family Man* swung gently about its mooring so it faced into the freshening wind.

The sun beat down on Cassie's arms and legs. The sky was a pale, milky white. A large seagull, its wings tipped in black, landed on top of the *Family Man's* cabin and stared at the empty food wrappers with a bright eye.

"I'm so full I could take a nap," Cassie said, rubbing her belly. "Thank you for lunch. I would've been feeling faint before I finished this installation. Now the afternoon will go much smoother."

Pauli smiled at her. "You're very welcome. Between eating half your sandwich and the incredible lasagna I felt I owed you."

Cassie lifted her face to the sun and closed her eyes. She'd take a few minutes to digest her sandwich before getting back to work. She felt relaxed and comfortable sitting on the wooden deck. Happy.

"Why won't you admit to me that you have *the sight?*"

Her happy bubble burst.

"What?!" No longer relaxed or comfortable, Cassie scrambled to her feet. She looked down at Pauli, still seated with his tanned legs stretched out in front of him and crossed at the ankles, his hands loosely clasped on his stomach.

He opened one blue eye and looked up at her. "I *know*. I know you see things from the near future. You saw Melody Harbush's accident, didn't you? And you saved that girl's life, the one who had an emergency appendectomy."

"How did you know about Sarah?"

"Is that the girl's name? Everyone was talking about how lucky she is that you noticed she didn't look well. But it was more than that, wasn't it Cassie?"

Cassie felt the blood drain from her head. She swayed on her feet.

"I *know*, Cassie, so you might as well talk to me about it."

"I can't." The words came out in a choked whisper.

Pauli opened both eyes and looked steadily at her. "Why can't you? I'm not going to call you crazy. And I'm definitely not going to tell anyone else about your visions. Tell me about them."

He patted the deck next to him and reached up a hand to help her sit. "Have a seat and talk to me. When did they start?"

Cassie stared blindly at the spot he patted, then sank to the deck where she stood, her legs suddenly too weak to support her. She swallowed several times before she could speak.

"How do you know . . . about—about the visions?"

"I recognize *the sight* in you because I have it too, although I don't think my visions are quite as intense or frequent as yours. Mine are more of a *knowing,* like intuition. You have the true *sight.* My gifts lie elsewhere."

"Gift? How can you call being crazy a gift?" Cassie's tone sounded bitter. "Nobody has ever believed me. The first one came when I turned thirteen. By then my mother was gone and it was only me and my dad. He thought I was making them up to get attention."

Pauli reached over and gently took one of Cassie's hands in his. He ran his thumb lightly over the back of her hand. "That must have been tough. At least in my family we expect this sort of thing so it's considered normal."

"You must have a very strange family then."

Pauli smiled. His blue eyes danced with laughter. "You could say that. It's brave of you to warn people like Melody Harbush even though they might call you crazy."

Pauli's big hand felt warm and safe, his thumb strokes soothing. Some of the tension left Cassie's body. She didn't understand why, but Pauli didn't seem the least bit bothered by her strangeness. It was a huge relief to finally talk to somebody about her visions without the risk of being called crazy.

"Sometimes I have to say something," she said slowly. "When the vision comes strong and I can see that somebody is going to be hurt. Like Mrs. Harbush. I saw her car in the ditch on its roof, and her bloody face. And Sarah MacDougal. I saw her in her bunk on their boat, deathly ill. I knew Sarah would die if her family took that cruise."

Pauli nodded. "You saved Sarah's life. How many listen to you and heed your warnings?"

"Sarah's mother, Myra MacDougal was the first." The seagull, finally realizing there was no food left for him, spread his wings and flew off the cabin with a raucous cry.

"Hmmm. That's interesting," Pauli said. "I wonder what changed?"

Cassie realized that he still held her hand and pulled it away. She immediately missed its warmth and wished she could put her hand back. "What do you mean, what changed? Nothing has changed."

"Something has, Cassie. Powers like *the sight* are usually tied to our karma and history. When something changes in our lives the power also changes. Your entire life, at least since you started having visions, nobody has believed you, right? Not one single person."

"N-no. I mean yes. You're right. Until Mrs. MacDougal no one has heeded my warnings. If I see them again after the vision comes true they treat me like I'm a witch, or something worse."

"Man's history has been peppered with seers, Cassie." Pauli wished she hadn't pulled her hand away. He liked holding it. She had a strong hand but her skin was soft and smooth, almost silky.

"Most probably kept their gift to themselves. You have a strong sense of duty and a desire to help people so you feel compelled to speak out. You need to figure out what changed in your life. Why did somebody believe you *then*. It's important."

The launch radio squawked and Pauli got smoothly to his feet. He reached down and grabbed Cassie by the upper arms and pulled her up.

"Think about it," Pauli said. "You can always talk to me. I won't judge you harshly. Not for that anyway."

Cassie saw his gaze focus on her mouth and knew that he intended to kiss her. She jerked her hand up in front of her face, then pushed against his chest.

"Oh no you don't."

"You sure? Kissing you feels right." He leaned his head closer to hers.

Cassie's blood began to thrum in her veins. She wanted Pauli to kiss her and that made her even more determined not to let him.

"Yes, I'm sure," she said, dismayed to hear the huskiness in her own voice. She took a deep breath and tried again. "I'm engaged to Brad, remember?"

"I don't see how that could have slipped my mind, seeing as how he made it clear that he's counting on us "commoners" to help him get elected to office." Pauli made no attempt to hide his sarcastic tone. He released his hold on Cassie and vaulted into the launch.

"Pauli responding to call at mooring three fifty-two. On my way," he replied into the radio. He motored off without a backward glance.

Goosebumps rose on Cassie's arms despite the warmth of the day. She rubbed them briskly with shaking hands. Her entire world had just shifted beneath her feet. She had admitted to having visions and Pauli hadn't even blinked an eye in surprise.

In fact, he had already suspected and had no problem believing her. And wasn't that strange and interesting? She'd like to meet his family. They had to be very different from normal families if they accepted something as bizarre as having visions as normal.

She refused to acknowledge the desire she'd felt when she realized Pauli wanted to kiss her. It simply wasn't right to want him when she was engaged to Brad. She wasn't the type of girl who fooled around.

She was a one-man woman, and she'd found her one man.

She pushed down the niggling doubt that she'd found the right one.

CHAPTER 11

"STAN, let's go out for pizza after work. What do you say?" Cassie placed her hand on Stan's meaty forearm. "You shouldn't lock yourself away from your friends."

Purple shadows and deep bags underneath Stan's bloodshot eyes told her the cutter hadn't been sleeping well since Doreen had walked out the week before.

"I'm not hungry. Besides, you really don't want to be with me. I'm not good company right now." Stan turned back to his work, stared at it for several moments, then just let his head hang.

Cassie saw tears leak out of his closed eyes. She grabbed one of his meaty hands in both of hers and gently squeezed.

"Stan. You need your friends around you to help you through this. I don't care if you don't speak a word to me through the entire meal. Have pizza with me. Brad's been working late practically every night for the last two months and I could use some company. Even silent company would be better than another meal alone."

Stan heaved a great sigh. "All right. But no scolding me or telling me I should've seen it coming."

Cassie patted his hand and let it drop. "Now why would I do that? You're a good husband, Stan. I'll meet you at Vinnie's Pizza at five-thirty. Does that work for you? I want to stop by my apartment and feed Handsome first but we should still be able to beat the dinner rush."

Cassie finished up her day's work and drove home to feed the cat. She didn't know if having dinner with Stan was the right thing to do, but she'd had another vision about Stan and Doreen a few nights ago and thought maybe she should tell him about it.

Doreen was going to go back to Stan. She had just needed some time to figure things out. One of those things that Doreen needed to realize was that she really did love Stan and didn't want to lose him.

Cassie didn't know if telling Stan was the right thing to do. What if her vision was wrong, or something happened and Doreen didn't go back to him after Cassie had raised his hopes?

On the other hand, Stan was really suffering. Every day he seemed to sink deeper into depression. He'd stopped eating and his clothes were beginning to sag off his large frame. He hadn't shaved and judging by the way he was beginning to smell, he hadn't bothered to shower either.

This was after only a week. What would he look like if Doreen took another month to come back?

What if Stan did something irreversible in the meantime—like take his own life rather than face life without the woman he loved? In the last day or two Cassie had begun to fear that Stan was thinking about suicide. She couldn't let that happen. Not when she felt fairly certain that Doreen was coming back to him.

She pulled into Vinnie's small, dirt parking lot and parked next to a Ford Bronco that had more rust than her old 4Runner. She was happy to see Stan's truck parked at the far left of the lot.

She could see Stan's bulk already seated in one of the two front windows, hunched over a tall glass of soda. He was playing with the straw, jabbing at the ice. Cassie pasted a smile on her face and breezed inside.

The mouth-watering scents of yeast, tomato, and Italian sausage greeted her. Vinnie's was a small, family-owned pizza and sandwich shop that catered to the local working class neighborhood. They offered tasty filling food at a fair price and did a great business.

Cassie wound her way through a mix of square and round cafe tables that sat on the black-and-white checkerboard floor and filled the front two-thirds of the shop.

The once red walls, now faded to a dull rose, were covered with framed movie posters from old black and white films. Bogart and Bacall in *Casablanca*. Grant and Hepburn in *Bringing Up Baby*. Myrna Loy and William Powell in *Mr. And Mrs. Thin Man*.

Cassie shared a love of old movies with the owner, Vincent Antania, and had won his lasting friendship when she discovered the Casablanca movie theater poster in a thrift shop and gifted him with it.

She approached the long counter that divided the eating area from the kitchen, greeting a couple of the regulars on the way. Behind the counter Cassie could see Vinnie tossing dough. A short, slight man with thick dark hair and warm brown eyes, he seemed to be the opposite of his quiet, round wife, Anna. Seeing the love between them usually brought a genuine smile to Cassie's face.

Anna spread sauce and toppings on two waiting pans, slid another pan into the oven beside her, and pulled two loaves of bread in front of her, deftly slicing them open.

"Cassandra! Buona Sera! Good evening!" Vinnie called to her. A wide smile split his handsome face. He gave the dough a final twirl and caught it in the waiting pan with a flourish.

Cassie clapped. "Brava, Vinnie. Hi, Anna. Has Stan already ordered?"

Anna shook her head. "No. He said he is not hungry. So sad, that one. I don't know what his wife is thinking. Stan is a good man. Good men are not that thick on the ground, you know?"

"Yeah, I know. Why don't you make us a large loaded? I'll try to get him to eat."

"You are a good friend, Cassie. We will make you a loaded."

Cassie grabbed a glass with ice and water and headed to Stan's table.

They talked about insignificant things while they ate. Or Cassie talked and ate while Stan merely grunted or answered in mono-syllables. He left his soda mostly untouched and Cassie ended up taking all but two slices of the pizza home with her. Fortunately she loved cold pizza.

She waited until they had paid and were outside in the parking lot to tell Stan about her recent vision.

"I think if you give Doreen some time and space that she's going to come back, Stan. I really do. She just needs to sort her feelings out."

Stan frowned at her. "You know that's not true, Cassie. Why would you even say something like that? Doreen is gone. Finis. End of my marriage to the only woman I've ever wanted."

Cassie hesitated, then decided What the hell? Stan was her friend.

"I-I see things sometimes, Stan. Remember the teenaged girl with appendicitis? I had a vision that she was going to get sick on the family's cruise. And early in the summer I *saw* that Doreen was leaving. A few days ago I *saw* that she would come back. What I *see* comes true. She still loves you."

Stan stared at his feet while Cassie talked. He gave no indication that he heard her words. When she finished he gave her a sad stare. "That's baloney. I don't believe in that vision crap.

Thanks for the invite for pizza. And thanks for trying to cheer me up. You're a good friend. Bye, Cassie."

He climbed into his big truck and peeled out of the parking lot, spraying dirt and small stones.

Cassie stared after him. She had tried. And because she had tried she shouldn't be feeling this badly that Stan had refused to listen. Doreen would return and all would be right with Stan's world again.

But all the way home Cassie was dogged with the feeling that she hadn't done enough to convince Stan.

She took a walk down to the estate dock with Handsome, a place that usually brought her peace, but she couldn't shake the sense of unease that she'd felt since parting with Stan.

She crawled into bed with a new romance but found herself reading the same paragraph over and over. Finally she gave up. She threw on some clothes and climbed back into her vehicle and drove over to Stan's house.

As soon as she turned down Stan's street she saw the flashing red and blue lights. Her prayer that they were for a neighbor died on her lips when she spotted the ambulance in Stan's driveway. She pulled to the curb and leaped from her vehicle.

Several of Stan's neighbors stood talking quietly on Stan's front lawn. Cassie ran over to them.

"I'm a friend of Stan's," she said. "We work together at the sail loft. What happened? Is Stan all right?"

A pudgy woman in a waitress uniform lifted one shoulder in a shrug. "We're not sure. I saw Doreen drive in about twenty minutes ago and ten minutes after that I heard the police and ambulance sirens. Someone must be ill."

"Thank you." Cassie saw the EMTs come out of the front door carrying a stretcher between them and hurried over. Her heart clenched when she saw Stan strapped to the stretcher, white-faced and unmoving under a blanket.

"Is he going to be all right? What happened?" she asked.

"Excuse us ma'am." The EMTs bulled past her and loaded Stan into the back of the ambulance, but not before Cassie saw a bandaged wrist flop out from under the blanket. One of the EMTs tucked it back inside the blanket. The doors closed and the ambulance took off with lights and siren blaring.

"Cassie." Doreen's face looked almost as white

as Stan's. She grabbed Cassie's arm. "Stan-he tried to kill himself. Oh god, if I hadn't come by he'd be dead. It's all my fault." Tears streamed down her face.

Cassie wrapped her free arm around Doreen's slim shoulders. "Would you like me to drive you to the hospital? You should be there when Stan comes to."

"Could you? Yes. Please. I-I could use the company. If Stan dies—"

"Stan is *not* going to die, thanks to you," Cassie said firmly. She sent up a silent prayer that she was telling Doreen the truth. "Close up the house and let's go."

Fifteen minutes later she paced the waiting room floor with Doreen. The room was empty other than a young couple sitting and talking quietly in a set of armchairs. A coffeepot sat on a small counter with styrofoam cups and powdered dairy. Cassie had poured a cup for Doreen but it smelled burnt so she'd passed on one for herself.

Stan was in surgery, and according to a nurse who they had stopped to question, was expected to fully recover, thanks to being found in time. They were sewing up his wrists and giving him a transfusion of blood and other fluids. Apparently

Stan had been neglecting to drink water as well as eat food and was severely dehydrated.

"This is all my fault," Doreen said for the hundredth time, wringing her hands. Tears leaked from her eyes. They were sitting in the chairs vacated by the young couple who'd headed down to the cafeteria.

"I never should have left. I just needed some time to myself to think, you know?" Doreen looked at Cassie with pleading eyes.

Cassie placed her hand over Doreen's and squeezed. "You did nothing wrong, Doreen. Taking time to think is no crime." She hesitated a moment. "Why were you at the house?"

Doreen grabbed a fresh tissue from the pack Cassie had produced from her backpack and blotted her tears. "I realized that I love Stan and we could work out our issues, but only if I was there to work them out. Running away wasn't the answer. I-I was hoping he'd take me back. My bags are in my car."

Cassie shook her head over the irony of the situation. If Stan had only listened to her. Or if he had just waited another hour before cutting his wrists. Then they'd all be spared this traumatic experience.

"Doreen? How is he?" Pauli came striding into

the room and went straight to Doreen. He lifted her from her chair and enfolded her in his arms. Doreen started sobbing, clinging tightly to Pauli's shirt.

Pauli looked at Cassie over Doreen's head. "How is Stan?" he asked again.

"He's going to make it," she replied. She felt ridiculously relieved to see Pauli. "He's in recovery now. They're pumping him with fluids because apparently he hasn't been drinking or eating. How did you know?"

"Think about it," was all Pauli said. He rubbed Doreen's back and made soothing noises until her sobs quieted, then led her back to her chair. Squatting in front of her, he took both her hands in his.

"Look at me." When Doreen raised her eyes to his Pauli reached back and pulled a folded bandana from his back pocket and handed it to her. "Wipe your face," he said gently.

With a half-laugh Doreen took the bandana and wiped her face.

"That's better. This is not your fault, Doreen. This is all on Stan. He loves you more than life itself. That can be hard to bear sometimes, being the recipient of that much love."

Doreen dabbed at her eyes and sniffled. "It is.

That's why I left. I felt overwhelmed by how much Stan loves me. I-I didn't know if it was fair. I love him, but I didn't know if I'd ever love him as much as he loves me. Our marriage felt lopsided. So I left."

"You came back." Pauli straightened and took the empty chair on Doreen's other side.

Doreen nodded. "Yes. I love Stan and I missed him terribly. And I realized that however much I love him seems to be enough for him."

"So maybe your marriage isn't as lopsided as you thought," Cassie said. "You're both getting what you need from it."

Pauli gave Cassie a quick, approving smile over Doreen's bowed head that ignited a small glow inside of her.

"You're right." Doreen's voice sounded stronger, calmer. "That's exactly right, Cassie. As long as we both feel that we're getting what we need then it's a good marriage. I just hope I get the chance to tell Stan."

Cassie patted Doreen's knee. "You will. Stan will be fine. Especially when he sees you. You're all he wants, Doreen. If he has you, he's a contented man."

Twenty minutes later the nurse came to take Doreen to see Stan. She thanked Cassie and Pauli and told them to leave as she was staying until the hospital discharged her husband.

Pauli escorted Cassie to her vehicle. "Why were you at Stan's?" he asked, leaning against the 4Runner with his arms crossed over his broad chest.

"I had a feeling. I met Stan for dinner at Vinnie's and he wouldn't eat. I went home but I couldn't stop worrying about him so I drove to their house. The ambulance was already there. How did you end up at the hospital?"

"I *saw* Stan bleeding and knew I'd better check it out. One of the neighbors told me the ambulance had taken him to the hospital and that Doreen rode in with a friend. I had a hunch it was you."

"You weren't lying about having visions."

"I *never* lie." The insult was clear in Pauli's voice.

Cassie moved to stand in front of Pauli. "Are we freaks?" she asked. She wanted the truth. If Pauli never lied he would tell her the truth.

Pauli snorted. "Definitely not. We have a special gift, that's all. That doesn't make us freaks any more than Beethoven's or Mozart's or Da Vinci's gifts made them freaks."

Cassie nodded. This was something she

needed to think about. "I can't imagine what it must feel like to be loved the way Stan loves Doreen," she said wistfully and immediately wished she hadn't spoken her thought aloud.

Pauli unfolded his arms and pulled her against him. He cupped her chin in one gentle hand and lowered his lips to hers. "That tells me that Brad Farland is not the right man for you," he whispered against her mouth, then kissed her long and deep.

Cassie was trembling from head to toe by the time Pauli ended the kiss. She leaned against Pauli's strong frame for several moments longer before pushing away and searching his eyes. Pauli's look never wavered.

"It's late," Cassie finally said. "I need to get to bed. Work tomorrow."

On the drive home she thought about degrees of love and wondered how one measured love. Was it better to be the one who loved more or the one who was loved?

These were questions she had no answer to.

CHAPTER 12

"YOU LOOK BEAUTIFUL TONIGHT, DARLING." Brad smiled down at Cassie.

"So do you." Brad did look incredibly handsome in his custom tux.

Cassie thanked the weather gods for the warm early August evening. She had waffled about bringing a wrap because of her bared left shoulder, but hadn't bothered since nothing in her closet looked right with the new-to-her silk dress.

They were making their way toward the event center's entry where the receiving line of the Summer Ball, held at Charlotte's club each August to raise money for different charities, waited in all their formal splendor.

Brad's mother had chaired the ball committee for the last twenty years and all around her Cassie could hear arriving guests wondering how Charlotte Farland managed to outdo herself year after year.

Cassie and Brad reached the bottom of the stairs leading into the event center. Above them both sets of double doors had been thrown open to the mild evening. A navy blue banner with pale gold lettering spanned the open doors, announcing that this was the forty-fifth Summer Ball.

They climbed the steps to the top and waited patiently for the group ahead of them to pass inside. Through the open doors Cassie could see a raised platform in one back corner of the large room. The platform held a small orchestra that was currently playing a quiet tune.

She couldn't hear it well enough over the chatter of the attendees around her to identify the composer but she recognized the music as classical. No rock and roll for this group, she mused.

Long narrow tables covered in deep blue cloths were set against the walls. Brad had told her that they held a variety of upscale items for the silent auction that would go on during the event—top bidders to be announced at the end.

The sail loft had donated a gift certificate for a new set of sails, a donation worth thousands of dollars. Cassie had been surprised at Jonathan's generosity until he told her that the donation always brought in at least a half dozen new customers who ended up covering the cost of the donated sails plus made the loft a profit.

She filed that information away for the following year when the Ball committee would need new auction items. She could donate a custom dodger or cushions. It was something to think about. She was always looking for clever ways to attract new customers.

She and Brad moved forward until they stood in the open doorway. Round tables circled the room inside the auction tables, leaving the center clear for dancing. Clothed in pale gold with the same deep navy underlayment, each table held a large cobalt glass vase filled with white hydrangeas.

Apparently Charlotte had chosen navy and gold for this year's color theme. Brad had told Cassie that his mother always started with her color scheme—it was one of the secrets to her success and reputation as top Summer Ball organizer.

Cassie's dress, a sleek column of navy silk that

she had scored last week from a consignment shop, would fit right in.

The line of guests now moved briskly forward, obviously anxious to get to the bar and silent auction.

"The receiving line makes me feel as if I'm attending an English ball," Cassie whispered in Brad's ear.

He smiled down at her. "That's the idea. The guests used to just arrive willy-nilly and mill around. Mother thought it would add some class and make the guests feel special if they were announced and met by the club's senior members."

Cassie hadn't realized they would be announced. Now she heard a man's voice boom out two names. She had heard the announcer as part of the background noise but hadn't paid attention. Would everyone look at them when their names were announced?

She straightened her shoulders and smoothed the silk with her free hand, a nervous gesture she knew, but she couldn't help herself. She *felt* nervous.

Fortunately she didn't have more than a few moments to think about it. They stepped inside the door, were announced as Brad Farland III and fiancee Miss Cassandra Brown.

She shook hands with several men and resisted the impulse to curtsy. She inclined her head instead toward Charlotte and a short round woman with obviously black-dyed hair and an abundance of diamonds draped over her person.

"Let's get some champagne and look over the auction offerings," Brad said as he led Cassie away from the receiving line and over to one of two bars that had been set up on opposite sides of the entry.

Cassie kept close to Brad's side and sipped at her champagne as they looked over the auction offerings, the majority of which were artworks and antiques. Oil and watercolor paintings, silver items, a variety of gift certificates, a set of finely carved wooden decoys, and an assortment of jewelry and sculptures crafted from various mediums covered the tables. Clipboards with lined forms for bidding numbers and amounts sat in front of each offering.

"Do you have a bidding number?" she asked.

"Of course. I need to bid on three or four and win at least one. Mother's orders. If you see anything that interests you let me know."

They moved down to what Cassie considered a particularly ugly oil painting that featured rows of dead pheasant hanging on the side of a wooden barn. Cassie suppressed a shudder and looked away from the painting. All those dead creatures made her feel depressed.

"Why do they use numbers and not names for bidding? I'd think that they'd raise more money if they got a little friendly competition between bidders going."

Brad grinned. "They used to do it that way, but one year the bidding got a little too competitive and a fight broke out. Very embarrassing for all concerned, you know. Mother switched to the anonymous bidding the following year. They don't raise quite as much but they preserve the club members' dignity."

Cassie shook her head and smiled back at him. "That's taking all the fun out of it. Think of the suspense everyone's missing out on wondering who's going to get into it over some tchotchke item."

"I'm with you."

The rumbling male voice came from behind Cassie's naked left shoulder. "Introduce me to your betrothed, Brad. She seems to have more common sense than your usual fare."

Brad looked up from the pheasant painting and smiled at the speaker. "Cassie, I'd like you to meet one of my oldest friends, Dr. Jay Bradford. Jay, this is Cassandra Brown."

Cassie turned and saw a tall, slim man with receding brown hair and twinkling eyes bracketed with fine lines. She held out her hand. His felt warm and dry, just like a doctor's should, she thought.

She smiled at him. "I'm pleased to meet any friend of Brad's, especially if you aren't a lawyer."

Jay barked out a laugh. "I really like this girl, Brad. See if you can hang on to her."

"Speaking of hanging on, where's Melinda?" Brad asked. "Don't tell me she finally wised up and divorced you?"

"Nah. She loves me too much. She's yakking it up with some friends at the table over there." Jay nodded toward a table half-filled with women. "You should join us when you're done spending all your unearned money here. Melinda would love to meet Cassie." He punched Brad lightly on the arm and wandered off.

"I like Dr. Bradford. I'd like to meet his wife. Can we sit with them?" Jay Bradford struck Cassie as down to earth and normal, someone she could be friends with. She suspected his wife was the same. Someone who didn't feel compelled to put on airs like most of the other women at the Ball.

Brad merely grunted as he wrote down his bidding number and an amount for the pheasant painting.

Cassie eyed it skeptically. "You really like that? The birds are all dead."

"It's called sporting art, and this was done by a collectible artist. It's worth a bid. Let's see what else we can find."

They finished touring the auction tables. Brad bid on a full day at Portland's premier day spa for Cassie and two more paintings before leading her to a table. Her spirits dropped when she saw Adam and Cherise sitting there with four other strangers.

Introductions were made. Besides Adam and Cherise the two men were also lawyers. One, a partner in Brad's firm, was there with his very lovely and much younger wife. The other attorney was a senior partner in a smaller but well-known firm. His wife looked bored and half drunk already. Her glassy mud brown eyes glossed over Cassie and dismissed her as unworthy.

Cassie looked longingly at Jay Bradford's

lively table and reluctantly took the chair Brad held out for her. He took the empty seat between Cassie and Cherise and the lawyers commenced to talking about the law.

Cassie sympathized with the senior partner's wife. If all she had to listen to was lawyer talk she might want to get drunk too. Unfortunately she sat between Brad and the senior partner and could do nothing but listen herself. It was rude to talk over them, not that the half-drunk wife looked the least bit interested in starting a conversation.

When a waiter came around with a tray of champagne flutes Cassie snagged one for herself. The senior lawyer's wife snagged two. Smart, Cassie thought, and hoped she wouldn't be driven to copying her.

The orchestra finished playing background classical music and began to play a livelier, danceable tune. Cassie loved to dance, but before she could ask Brad to take her out onto the floor, Cherise grabbed his hand and led him out.

Cassie tried not to feel hurt and angry, but she couldn't help but resent Cherise. And Brad. He should've told Cherise that he wanted to dance the first dance with Cassie.

The other men were still deep in their lawyerly conversation. She listened for a couple minutes and realized she couldn't bear another minute sitting there. If she couldn't dance at least she could move around the room.

She stood, intending to make her way to the Bradford table. She would be brave and introduce herself to the doctor's wife. But on the way to their table she lost her nerve and detoured to the ladies room instead.

She just needed a moment she told herself, a moment to check that she looked okay and gather her courage to approach a table filled with strangers.

Unsurprisingly, the washroom turned out to be large and well-appointed with a carpeted seating area, an attendant, and plenty of roomy stalls. A dozen women primped and gabbed in front of the long counter and wall mirror.

Cassie recognized the haughty blonde at the mirror from the day she and Amber had met with Mavis Franks. She ignored her and headed for the bathroom stalls.

"It's Cassandra Brown, right? Aren't you Brad Farland's fiancee?"

The conversations around her died out as everyone strained to hear. Cassie met the blonde's smirking eyes in the mirror. She nodded curtly. "Yes. Excuse me."

But the blonde had no intention of letting Cassie go. She turned away from the mirror and raised her voice slightly, making sure even the women in the lounge area would hear her every word.

"Nice dress. It looks exactly like the one I wore to last season's Summer Ball. I believe that it's important to keep current in fashion, so I dropped that dress off at a *consignment* shop this spring." She waited, her eyes filled with malice, to see what Cassie would do.

Despite shaking inside, Cassie smiled at her. "It must have been difficult to let go of such a beautiful dress. I'm sorry to hear that you needed the money."

She turned away from the blonde's expression of outrage and entered the nearest stall, closed the door and leaned her forehead against the smooth cool metal while she took several breaths to steady herself. She heard several soft guffaws and titters from the other women.

It took several minutes for Cassie to feel able to leave the stall and face whoever was still in the washroom. She flushed the john even though she hadn't used it, and made her way to the sinks without looking at anyone.

"I'd like to be the first to applaud you for what you said to Clarissa. She's such an unpleasant bitch. You're the first person I've heard actually best her. That was a clever put-down."

The woman waited for Cassie to dry her hands before holding out one of her own. She had a firm handshake, not the limp, you're-lucky-I-let-you-touch-me handshake of the other women Cassie had met at the Ball.

"I'm Melinda Bradford. You've already met my husband, Jay. He liked you and I can see why."

Cassie smiled, a real smile this time. "I'm so glad to meet you. I liked your husband, too. I was actually on my way to your table when I popped in here. I wouldn't have bothered if I'd known Clarissa—is that her name?—was in here."

"I'm glad you didn't know. You would have deprived several of us of the best entertainment of the Ball. I predict you'll be famous within twenty minutes. And for what it's worth, the dress looks much nicer on you than it did on Clarissa."

Cassie blushed. "That's very kind of you."

Melinda hooked her arm through Cassie's and led her from the bathroom. "Come on. I'll introduce you to the more down to earth and fun guests. I promise you'll fit right in with us."

She led Cassie to a table filled with smiling, laughing people. One of the men jumped up and offered Cassie his chair.

"Oh, I can't take your seat," she protested.

"Not to worry. I'll grab an empty chair and squeeze it in," he said with a warm smile. "Besides, my wife is dying to hear about your meet with the infamous witch Clarissa."

A redhead with sparkling green eyes patted the empty chair. "That's right. Word travels fast around here and word has it that you put the club's top witch in her place. Sit. I'm Anne. The gallant gentleman who gave you his seat is my husband Charlie."

Cassie blushed but took the seat. "Thank you. I-I don't know what to say."

"You're embarrassing the girl, Anne. I was standing right there. I'll tell you every wonderful detail," Melinda said.

The entire table hooted when Melinda relayed how Clarissa had stormed out of the ladies room after Cassie's zinger.

"High five there, sister," said a dark-haired Asian woman. "Clarissa has been a thorn in my side ever since her daddy bought her a membership in the club. If it was up to her all members would be blonde and white. I'm Lin, by the way. I work with Jay at his pediatrics practice."

Charlie returned with a chair then and introductions were finished around the table. A flute of champagne appeared in front of Cassie. The talk flitted around a variety of subjects from children to camping and hiking and eventually veered to boats.

By the time Brad showed up to claim her Cassie had made several appointments to look at replacing old canvas.

"They were fun," Cassie said as she reluctantly followed Brad back to their table.

"They're okay. You made a good impression on them and I appreciate that. They'll be more likely to donate to my upcoming campaign. I wish you wouldn't conduct business here though. That's considered tacky."

Cassie stopped.

Brad took several steps, realized she was no longer following him, and turned back. "What?"

"I didn't make friends with them because of your political aspirations, Brad. I genuinely like them. They're warm, friendly, down to earth people. My kind of people. And *they* brought up the canvas work, not me."

Brad took her arm and spoke quietly into her ear. "Don't make a scene, Cassie. You're right. They are good people. And they happen to have money that I'd like to see backing me instead of my opponent when the time comes. That's all I meant. Let's dance."

Cassie let him lead her away from the tables to the dance floor. As they danced she relaxed in Brad's arms. Maybe she *had* overreacted a little bit. Running for governor was a big deal that took mega-planning. Of course it was often on Brad's mind.

She made it through the remainder of the evening sitting at the lawyer table. Managed to speak a few words with the young trophy wife and wished she hadn't when the woman went on and on about shoes.

As they were leaving they saw Lin getting into her car. Cassie went rigid as a vision of Lin being attacked by a burglar in her home flashed in her brain.

"I have to speak to Lin a minute," she told Brad as she pulled away from him and hurried toward Lin's car. She knocked on the window and Lin lowered it with a smile.

"It was great to meet you—" Lin began.

"Don't go straight home. Or at least take

someone with you," Cassie interrupted. How could she tell this woman that she was in danger? "Please. I-I have a horrible feeling that something's going to happen to you."

Lin gave her a strange look, then shrugged. "Is this an intuition thing? My mother is a strong believer. Don't worry, I'll be careful, I promise. It was nice meeting you, Cassie." She rolled up her window and drove off.

"What was that all about?" asked Brad when she joined him.

"Oh. I just wanted to tell Lin that I enjoyed meeting her."

Preoccupied with worry about Dr. Bradford's co-worker Lin, Cassie spoke little on the way home. She gave Brad a brief kiss when he parked next to her SUV.

"Thanks. The Ball was lovely. Your mother did a great job. And I'm glad you won the bid on your sporting art."

"It's a nice piece to add to my collection. I'll call you when I can. I'm afraid I'm going to be working a lot of late nights before the wedding, trying to get ahead of my caseload so we can take that three week honeymoon I promised you. You understand."

Cassie smiled. "Of course. I know you're a big

shot lawyer and I understand about work. We'll see more of each other after the wedding when we'll be living together."

She ran up the stairs to her apartment and let herself in, kicking off her high heels with relief. Handsome greeted her with loud meows and bumped against her shin. She picked him up and buried her face in his fur.

Lin had seemed to take her warning seriously. And now that Cassie had time to think about it, why had she? What made Lin different from the scores of others who had brushed off her warnings? Was it simply that Lin's mother believed in intuition?

Until tonight Myra MacDougal had been the only person who had ever believed her and done something about it. Only two people out of hundreds. Why those two? Why now? Something told Cassie that it was important for her to figure out the answer.

She hoped Lin wouldn't tell the others about her warning. She had really liked Jay and Melinda and their friends.

She wandered to the window and looked out at the lights twinkling through the trees from the bay's inhabited islands. She had seen the vision. And they always came true.

Lin would surprise a burglar if she ignored Cassie's warning and entered her home. Cassie could only pray he didn't hurt her too badly.

She set Handsome down and began to pace, then placed a phone call.

CHAPTER 13

CASSIE HUNG onto one of her stainless steel dodger frames, trying not to fall between the rocking boats. Other hulls knocked against the boat in the strong wind. How could that be? The marina took great pains to carefully space the boat moorings to prevent them from ever touching their neighbors.

Bang! Bang! Snapping canvas and sails sounded like pistol shots. The sailboat rocked violently beneath her and she lost her footing. She swung out over the water with one hand hanging onto the metal frame.

She would be crushed between the hulls if she fell. How long would it be before someone noticed her missing and came to look for her?

With a huge effort she pulled herself onto the sailboat's deck and sank to her knees, trembling with relief. She was safe.

Bang! Bang! Bang!

This time the noise penetrated her brain. She opened her eyes in confusion and saw that she was safe in her bed. The pounding continued. It took her another few moments to realize that someone was pounding on her door.

She crawled out of her bed and grabbed the light seersucker robe she used for warm summer nights.

"Coming! I'm coming," she muttered, and almost tripped over Handsome as he raced her down the stairs. She stopped to flip on a lamp by the couch and hit the switch for the light over the door.

"Who is it?" she asked through the door.

"Cassie. It's Pauli, let me in. Hurry."

"Pauli? What are you doing here? Jeezus, it's two in the morning."

"I know what time it is. Let me in. Hurry. They're almost here."

"Who's almost here?" Cassie asked as she unlocked the door.

Pauli yanked it open and stepped inside, crowding Cassie back. He switched off the entryway light, crossed to the lamp and turned it off, plunging the apartment into darkness.

"I repeat, what are you doing here? Why'd you turn off the lights?" She felt irritated now and a little frightened. After all, she didn't know Pauli all that well and he was definitely exhibiting bizarre behavior.

Pauli came back and closed the door, sliding the deadbolt home. He kicked off his shoes and hung his windbreaker on a peg. "Find me a blanket and a pillow, quick. *Move it*, Cassie. They're right behind me."

Cassie planted her feet and crossed her arms. "I'm not getting you anything until you tell me what's going on."

Pauli grabbed her by the arms and gave her a little shake. "The police are here for you. *That's* what's going on. Now hurry up and toss me down a blanket and pillow, then wait in the loft."

"Police? Why are they—"

Pauli gritted his teeth. "*Now*, Cassie. Do as I say *now*." He pulled his tee shirt off and stuffed it in the windbreaker pocket, then mussed his hair.

Cassie heard heavy feet on the stairs. What were the police doing here?

"Dammit. I didn't get here quick enough. I tried to save your reputation. Remember that."

A new fist pounded on Cassie's door. "Cassandra Brown? This is the police. Open up."

Pauli pushed Cassie behind him. He turned and whispered softly into her ear. "Shhh. Don't say anything. And don't move." He stepped lightly over to the couch, pulled a bright throw off and wrapped it around his shoulders.

Cassie's heart thumped hard in her chest. What was going on?

The pounding on the door resumed. "Cassandra Brown. Open up. This is the police."

"Hang on, hang on," Pauli called loudly. He stomped to the door, turned on the entry light and opened the door a crack. "Do you have identification?" he asked.

"Yes. If you'll open the door we'll be happy to show you."

"Slide it through. For all I know you could be robbers."

He checked the two ids and opened the door wider, wrapping an arm around Cassie's shoulder. "What's going on? Why are you here?" he asked.

"Cassandra Brown?"

Cassie nodded. "Yes." Her voice cracked. Even though she'd been raised to trust the police, she felt afraid. What reason could they have to come to her door at this time of night?

"We'd like to ask you a few questions."

"About what?" Thank heavens Pauli was there and holding onto her. Cassie wasn't sure her legs could support her, they were shaking so hard.

"May we come in?"

Unsure of how to answer, Cassie looked up at Pauli.

"Of course." Pauli stepped out of the way and led Cassie to a chair at the table. He pulled it out for her and gently pushed her into it.

The officers followed them and each took a seat facing Cassie.

"Can we get you officers something to drink?" Pauli asked.

"No, thank you. Miss Brown, I'm Detective Hazlett. I'm going to read you your rights."

Her rights? Was she under arrest? She felt Pauli's hand on her shoulder. Thank heaven he was there. Why were the police reading her her rights? That's what they did when they arrested someone. Wasn't it? She tried to swallow the lump in her throat.

"Do you know a Dr. Edwards, Miss Brown?"

Cassie shook her head no.

"Are you sure? She claims she knows you."

"I-I don't have any customers by that name. It's not familiar."

"Where were you this evening, Miss Brown?"

"I went to the Summer Ball with my fiancé Brad Farland. Oh! Dr. Edwards! Yes!" Cassie nodded her head vigorously. "You mean Lin. I met a woman named Lin there. Dark hair, Asian ancestry. Is that her? Why do you ask?"

"She surprised a burglar in her house tonight when she returned from the Ball." The detective watched Cassie closely. "He hit her with a heavy statuette and knocked her out. Fortunately someone had made an anonymous call to the station and said there was a burglar in her neighbor's house. A pair of patrolmen arrived on the scene before he could hurt Dr. Edwards any worse."

Relief flooded Cassie's body. She sagged in the chair. "She's going to be all right then?"

"Yes, thanks to the caller. Unfortunately the burglar got away and the caller didn't identify herself so we can't find out what she saw. Dr. Edwards told us you tried to warn her about the burglar, Miss Brown, and we're wondering how you knew about him."

Cassie felt the blood drain from her face. She felt woozy and ill. Did the detective believe she had played a part in the burglary? What could she tell him?

"I-I don't think I can answer that."

Detective Hazlett's expression hardened. "Why did you warn Dr. Edwards not to go home, Miss Brown? What did you know? Do we need to take this in to the station?"

"I didn't *know* anything." Cassie wrung her hands together. Pauli took the seat next to her and put his arm around her shoulder. She leaned into him, grateful for the support. "You're not going to believe me when I tell you."

"Try us." The second detective's tone was dry. "You wouldn't believe some of the stories we hear."

"It's not a story. It's the truth." Anger cleared out the woozy, ill feeling and made Cassie feel stronger. She straightened her body.

"Sometimes I get these premonitions. I had one tonight about Lin and I told her to be careful. Apparently she didn't believe me and went straight home."

"Premonitions?" The second detective looked incredulous. "Are you trying to tell us you're like —" he leaned forward and waggled his eyebrows "—a psychic?"

Cassie gave the second detective a cool look. "I'm sorry, I didn't catch your name."

"Detective Perlmann. Let's just cut to the meat here. Were you working with the burglar, Miss Brown?"

"No and no. I'm not psychic and I would never steal. I get these visions now and then. I had one a few weeks ago about a young girl getting deathly ill and I told her mother. She felt concerned enough to have a doctor check her daughter out. The daughter had appendicitis."

Detective Hazlett took a bent notebook and a stubby pencil from his shirt pocket. "Name?"

"MacDougal. Myra MacDougal is the mother. Sarah is the daughter."

"I would never steal, Detective," Cassie repeated. "I believe in earning what I want, not taking from others. The premonition I had about Lin was very strong, so strong that I felt I had to say something, even though it probably made her wonder if I was crazy. I don't like people to think I'm crazy. I would never have said anything if the feeling hadn't been so strong."

Both detectives looked at Cassie long and hard. Finally Detective Hazlett put his little notebook away and stood. "Thank you for your time,

Miss Brown. Don't leave town in case we have any further questions."

Pauli escorted them to the door, then returned to the table. He took Cassie's hand and led her to the couch, drew her down beside him. "Tell me what happened," he said.

"They didn't even ask who you were. What will Brad say if he finds out I had a man in my apartment at two in the morning?"

"He won't find out. Tell me about Dr. Edwards and the vision."

Instead of answering, Cassie frowned at Pauli. "How did you know the police were coming to see me?"

Pauli sighed. "I told you that I have visions, same as you. I had one tonight. I knew the cops were coming here and I knew why. You made the anonymous call about the burglary didn't you?"

Cassie nodded. "I couldn't go to bed without doing something about it. I felt afraid for Lin. She struck me as a very independent and strong woman, one who wouldn't think twice about facing down a robber."

Handsome batted at her naked toes and she leaned down to scoop him up with her free hand. "The vision was strong and very clear." She described what she'd seen to Pauli.

It comforted her to know that he believed her. She remembered that he had told her that he *saw* Stan in trouble the night he came to the hospital. Now tonight he had come to help her because he *saw* the police here.

It comforted her even more to realize that he really did have visions and hadn't just told her that to make her feel better.

She shifted sideways to look at him. "You really do have visions. Like I do."

Pauli nodded, his blue eyes fastened on hers, but didn't say anything.

She thought back to their conversation on the *Family Man*. "And your family knows about them?"

"Yes."

"Did they send you to see a shrink when you told them?"

The corner of Pauli's mouth kicked up. "No. Seers are common in my family. For us it's like having blue eyes or great physical strength. Just another genetic trait."

"Are you fortune tellers?"

Now Pauli's eyes twinkled at her. "No. We are definitely not fortune tellers."

He decided it was time to change the subject. "I know that Dr. Edward's brother-in-law burgled her place. I'm going to follow your lead and call in an anonymous tip tomorrow. Once they catch him they'll forget all about you."

"Her brother-in-law?" Cassie repeated, eyes wide. "That's just awful. What a lousy thing to do to anybody, let alone family."

"I agree. He won't get away with it, I promise you."

The throw had slipped off Pauli's shoulders when he sat on the couch. Cassie found herself staring at his bare, well-muscled and tanned torso. She clenched her hands in Handsome's fur in an effort to resist the sudden temptation to run her palms over the light mat of chest hair.

Desire warmed her and pooled in her abdomen. She raised her eyes to Pauli's face and found him watching her, all amusement gone from his expression. Heat lit his beautiful eyes.

Cassie swallowed. She was having trouble catching her breath. She stood abruptly. Handsome gave an unhappy yowl as he was dumped to the floor.

"I should get back to bed," Cassie said, her voice whispery. She cleared her throat. "Thank you for coming over. I don't think I could have handled the detectives without you."

Pauli grabbed her hand and pulled her down

into his lap before she could step away. He wrapped an arm around her waist and cupped her chin with his free hand.

"Cassie. Look at me."

Cassie kept her eyes down. She shook her head. "I don't want to," she whispered. "You're dangerous to me."

"Look at me."

Against her will Cassie raised her eyes.

"There's something between us, Cassie," Pauli said. He watched her closely. "Something very powerful and good. I know you feel it. I want you to know it's something I've never felt with any other woman. You're very special."

Cassie's body felt heavy and achy and oh so right snuggled up to Pauli. A great yearning to be touched and fondled by the man holding her nearly overwhelmed her.

She shook her head slightly. "I'm engaged. There can't be anything between us." Her voice didn't sound like her own. She repeated her comment, trying to put some force behind it.

She tried to pull her chin free but Pauli lowered his face and softly pressed his warm lips to hers. Cassie felt flames shoot up from her toes to her scalp. She shuddered.

"Cassie." Pauli whispered her name against her

mouth. "You undo me." He wrapped both arms around her and kissed her again, much more thoroughly.

Cassie moaned. She wanted to wrap herself around Pauli, wanted to taste him all over. Wanted to make love to him. It took all of her will power to place her hands flat against Pauli's perfect chest and push.

"I can't," she gasped, and tumbled off his lap when he unexpectedly released her.

They stared at each other, both breathing hard. After a long moment Pauli took a deep breath and let it out on a heavy sigh, then nodded and stood. "Of course you can't. You're an honest woman."

He picked Cassie off the floor and set her on her feet, then walked to the door and put on his tee shirt and jacket.

He opened the door but didn't step through. He looked over his shoulder to where Cassie stood still as a marble statue. More beautiful than any work of art.

"Maybe you're engaged to the wrong man, Cassie," he said quietly. "A truly honest woman would think about that."

The door closed quietly behind him.

ONE WEEK HAD PASSED since the Summer Ball and Pauli's parting words. Words that had filled Cassie with an uncertainty she didn't want to think about. Words she couldn't *stop* thinking about. They bobbed underneath the surface like a dull headache that couldn't be ignored.

Pauli didn't know what he was talking about, she told herself for the thousandth time as she matched a cushion top with the bottom and fed it through her sewing machine.

Pauli knew nothing about her relationship with Brad. What happened between them that night had simply been a reaction to being interrogated by the Portland detectives in the middle of the night.

Just because Pauli's kiss took her breath away . . . no, she wasn't going there. Cassie jerked her head and muttered to herself. So what if Pauli was an amazing kisser? It only meant that he'd had lots of practice.

The wedding was in five weeks. She had made a commitment to Brad and she was getting married. Pauli was nothing more than a friend and she intended to keep it that way. He'd be leaving Portland in a short while anyway once the boating season wrapped up.

Cassie stepped firmly on the part of her that was screaming for more Pauli and closed it away.

As Pauli had predicted, the police forgot about Cassie when Dr. Lin Edward's brother-in-law was arrested for robbing her house and attacking her. To Cassie's relief there was no mention of her premonition in the Portland Press Herald's story on the robbery.

Her upcoming wedding to Brad on the other hand had become almost daily fodder for the paper's society page. Charlotte called Cassie every day with wedding or reception updates and instructions for phone interviews with Maddy Stowe, the top society reporter for the Press Herald.

Maddy Stowe called nearly as often as Charlotte, looking for tidbits on the wedding plans. In the last few days Cassie had taken to checking her caller id before answering her phone.

Much to Cassie's chagrin, Charlotte had a carefully worked out publicity campaign for Brad's run for governor and Cassie played a large role.

Getting a job with the state's most prestigious law firm was step one.

Accomplished.

Make partner—not *just* partner, but the *youngest* partner ever—step two.

Almost there. The partnership had been promised to Brad right after the wedding.

Keep Brad's name in front of the public until the name Brad Farland III became a household name.

Underway.

Maddy Stowe published stories about Cassie being fitted for her dress, stories about choosing the flowers in her bridal bouquet and the flowers for the church and reception hall, stories about choosing the reception china and cutlery, the orchestra, the engraved invitations.

It went on and on until Cassie wanted to beg Brad to elope with her. They could go to Vegas and avoid the hoopla. That was an impossible dream of course. Brad would never disappoint his mother.

Charlotte called and fed the wedding details to Cassie, Maddy interviewed Cassie and printed her fluff pieces, and Brad's name was in front of the voters. All according to plan.

In Cassie's mind the stories Charlotte planted through her society writer friend were in bad taste. They flaunted the Farland money in the faces of those less fortunate and that made Cassie feel uncomfortable.

Not to mention that the stories were essentially lies as Cassie herself had very little to do with the wedding plans. They were all being orchestrated behind the scenes by Charlotte. Cassie was basically just a yes man—or in this case a yes woman.

When Cassie tried to speak with Charlotte about the news stories she got nowhere.

"You have no experience with this kind of thing," Charlotte had said coolly, dismissing Cassie's concerns with a wave of her ringed and manicured hand. "It's expected of us. Brad's wedding is the social event of the year and people want to read everything about it. Maddy's pieces are the perfect vehicle to get his name in every household. We need to reach the woman voters as well as their husbands, you understand. No woman can resist a wedding."

Brad's wedding. Charlotte referred to the wedding as "Brad's wedding." Not "your" wedding. Cassie was beginning to understand that agreeing to let Charlotte have her way about the ceremony and reception had been a bad idea. If only she had realized then that Brad's mother's only goal in life was to get her son into the governor's mansion.

The planted stories got so bad that Cassie started skipping that section of the paper. Unfortunately Amber had taken to reading the society page religiously and informed Cassie daily of the latest.

"According to the paper your wedding is going to be the event of the year, possibly of the decade," Amber crowed during their coffee break one morning.

Cassie had finished her morning's project on autopilot, her mind elsewhere, like driving a route you knew so well that when you arrived at your destination you realized you didn't recall any details of the trip.

"I don't want to hear it," Cassie grumbled.

Amber grinned. The recent tension Cassie had sensed in her friend had disappeared since Amber had started dating Tyler. The shop owner apparently doted on Amber and her friend was flourishing under his attentions.

A small jolt of jealousy stabbed at Cassie. Amber and Tyler dined together nearly every night after the work day, slept together either at Amber's or Tyler's apartment over his shop, and spent their free time doing stuff together.

Cassie on the other hand, hadn't seen Brad since the Summer Ball and only had short phone conversations with him. She understood the pressure he was under to do well at his law firm and to make partner, but she felt lonely.

"How's Tyler's business doing?" she asked, trying to change the subject. It worked like a charm. Amber was off and running about some new pieces Tyler had discovered at a recent estate sale. Despite her foul mood Cassie found herself interested and she felt lighter after their break.

Maine was enjoying an exceptionally warm and dry August with a mild September forecast. Predictions were for an extra-colorful fall foliage season and a record high number of tourists flocking to the state. Boaters were arranging to leave their craft in the water through the fall, extending the season as long as possible.

Unfortunately, the sail loft's workload was already dropping off. The frenzy of May and June, the two months when the majority of people thought about freshening and updating old canvas and sails, had slowed to a steady work flow through July and into early August.

The extra stitcher Jonathan had hired had already been let go. The wild pace of high summer had dropped to the steady hum of late summer. There was time for coffee breaks and conversation.

Stan had returned to work only that week. He could only manage part time but Cassie was glad to see him happy again now that Doreen had moved back into their home.

He had cornered Cassie his first day back and given her a big hug, thanking her for trying to help him during his "bad spell" and apologizing for causing her so much trouble.

Touched, Cassie had patted Stan on the arm and told him there was no need for apologies. They were friends and friends looked out for one another.

As August drew to a close the sail loft shifted into winter hours. The slower pace gave Cassie far too much time to think and she hated it. While she had managed to avoid being alone with

Pauli since the night of the police visit, she couldn't hide from her own thoughts.

"What's wrong with you?"

"What?" Amber's question jolted Cassie from her thoughts. "Nothing. Why do you think something's wrong with me?"

Amber narrowed her green eyes at Cassie. "I've asked you twice now if you'd like to come with me to Tyler's shop after work to see some new art deco lamps he picked up this week. Obviously your mind was someplace else. Thinking about the big day?"

"Big day?"

"Jesus, Cassie. Your wedding. You know, the day you become Mrs. Bradford Farland the Third?"

"Oh, that big day." Cassie walked over to the loft's small corner sink and dumped the remains of her cold tea and rinsed out her cup.

"Cassie, what's wrong?"

The women were alone in the loft. Stan had left for the day and Jonathan was off conferring with the marina's bookkeeper.

"Nothing's wrong. Not really," Cassie answered, not looking at her friend.

"Cassie." Amber walked over to join Cassie

and placed a freckled hand on her shoulder. "What's wrong? You can tell me."

Cassie took a deep breath. She needed to talk to somebody about the things churning her up inside. She took a second breath.

"Deep down, *way* deep down," she said softly, "a tiny voice is telling me that Brad comes from a different world than I do, a privileged world unlike anything I'm familiar with. I'm afraid that I'll never get the hang of being Mrs. Brad Farland."

"The Third," Amber added with a grin.

Cassie scowled. "Yeah, yeah. The Third."

Amber ran her hand down Cassie's arm. "There's more, isn't there?"

Cassie nodded. "I don't know if I even *want* to become part of Brad's world," she admitted.

Amber gripped Cassie's wrist. "Cassie, that's pretty serious. You need to be sure. Do you love him?"

It occurred to Cassie that she didn't really know Brad all that well. They had met in a small, local coffee shop on Rt. 88 when both had been in a hurry to get to work. Brad had grabbed her order by mistake and Cassie had chased him down in the parking lot to get her coffee and scone.

They had laughed at the mix-up and Brad had

asked her out to dinner. She had liked his handsome, square-jawed face and hazel eyes and said yes, not knowing then that he was Brad Farland III, Portland's most eligible bachelor.

They had dated for six months, then he had asked her to marry him. Cassie had been flattered and a little in awe that a catch like Brad would want to marry a nobody like her. She'd said yes.

Brad had worked long hours six and seven days a week for most of that dating period. Cassie herself had been working almost as much for several of those months. It hadn't left a lot of time to spend getting to know each other.

And of course Brad had never once stayed overnight at Cassie's or asked her to spend the night at his place.

"I'm pretty sure I do," Cassie answered. "He's everything I've ever dreamed of in a husband. He's handsome, intelligent, and hard-working."

"And very, very wealthy," Amber added with a smirk.

"True. But I didn't know he had money until right before he proposed to me." Cassie looked at Amber. "You know the money doesn't matter to me, right?"

Amber cleaned her coffee mug and hung it on its hook. "I know you aren't a gold digger, Cassie.

But you do realize that people will think you're marrying Brad for his money, don't you?"

"Other women might find Brad's money and social standing a huge plus, but I'm beginning to think it's a huge minus. Brad's entire lifestyle insulates him from most of the world, including me." Cassie cringed inwardly at the bitter tone she heard in her voice.

What if she had made a mistake? Had she been swept away by the magic of having someone tell her he loved her and her first marriage proposal?

How could he ever really understand her?

And that thought tracked in both directions. Could she ever really understand him?

Cassie felt out of her comfort zone in Brad's world. He and Charlotte repeatedly told her she would get used to it but she wondered how long that would take.

As Brad's wife she would be expected to host dinner parties for people she had zero in common with. And what if he really did run for governor and won? Could she deal with being the governor's wife?

Cassie grabbed her friend's arm, an expression of panic on her face. "What if Brad gets elected governor, Amber? What will I do then? I can't be a governor's wife! I'm not trained for that sort of thing. I'm a canvas worker, not a politician's wife."

"Have you talked to Brad about all this, Cassie? You really ought to let him know how you feel."

"I tried." When she had voiced her misgivings to Brad during the one dinner they had shared since the Summer Ball, he patted her hand and told her not to worry, that his mother would be there to help her learn the ropes.

"He told me not to worry. Charlotte will help me."

Amber snorted. "Mmmm, wonderful woman your future mother-in-law."

Cassie groaned. Charlotte was another whole issue. Brad's mother was so . . . efficient and driven that Cassie had to admit she felt intimidated by her. She couldn't imagine they would ever develop a warm mother/daughter relationship, something Cassie had always hoped to gain once she was married.

"You need to talk to Brad," Amber repeated. "Go over there tonight and tell him everything you just told me. Force him to really listen to your feelings."

"Okay," Cassie said. She nodded. "Okay. That's what I'll do. I'll go see Brad."

ANOTHER WEEK SLID by and Cassie still hadn't voiced her doubts to Brad—mostly because he hadn't had time to see her. This wasn't something she felt she could discuss over the phone. She needed to see his eyes, see his facial expressions, his body language. So much of communication was non-verbal.

No, a phone conversation wouldn't cut it.

In the meantime the fear that she should never have accepted Brad's proposal continued to grow.

Cassie had her final fitting with the dress maker on the Friday evening two weeks before the wedding. She had to admit that the dress Charlotte had chosen looked absolutely stunning.

She stared at her reflection with a sense of

awe. Her tanned, toned shoulders were bared while her arms were covered in the smooth ivory silk, the sleeves ending in points that partially covered the backs of her hands.

Delicate seed pearls, sewn on by hand, covered the bodice and modest train and the sleeve points. The dress glowed with reflected light and made her look like a fairy tale princess.

Cassie had tried to choose a simpler dress, one that fit within her budget, but Charlotte had been adamant about the one of a kind designer dress and overruled her.

"It's beautiful," Cassis said to the designer. He beamed at her. She turned to her future mother-in-law. "You were right. The dress is incredible."

"Of course I was right. Don't ever forget that you have an image to uphold, Cassie," Charlotte reminded her. "Besides, Brad is paying for the dress and he expects his future wife to choose the best. Brad can easily afford to have his wife wear the finest available. He'll expect it of you."

Cassie caught the underlying message in Charlotte's words. After the wedding she would be expected to look like a Farland.

She had reluctantly agreed to the dress. She hated that Brad was paying for her dress *and* the wedding—those were supposed to be the bride's responsibility—but she would have had to sell everything she owned to raise enough money just for the deposit on one sleeve of the dress Charlotte had chosen.

Cassie's nerves kicked into high gear as she viewed herself in the dressmaker's mirrors. Very soon she, Cassandra Brown of the poor and essentially unremarkable Browns, would be taking up a new position in the eye of the public.

The wedding would catapult her into that position. She would never be simply Cassie Brown again.

Looking at herself in the mirror as the dressmaker messed with one of the sleeve points, Cassie realized that the simple dress she had originally chosen would have been embarrassing to the Farland's social standing.

From this point forward that was something she needed to be aware of. Was she capable?

The event hall, the decorators, the florists, the caterers, the liquor, the band, the photographer, the gifts for the attendees—all had been paid for. There could be no backing out now.

In two weeks Cassandra Brown would become Cassandra Farland III. She should feel excitement. She should be glowing with happiness.

So why did she feel a knot in her stomach that

grew larger and harder to ignore as the wedding grew closer?

Later that night, Cassie poured her second glass of wine and stared at her reflection in her apartment window. She had lost weight. She hadn't bothered to blow dry her hair that day and curls bounced everywhere. Her eyes looked worried and haunted.

Before she could think twice about it she set the wineglass on the dining table and grabbed her bag and keys. She needed to talk to Brad and she needed to speak with him in person.

She hadn't seen him other than the one dinner they'd shared since the Summer Ball. He was beginning to feel like a stranger to her. Cassie saw more of Brad's mother then she did of her fiancé.

She ran down her steps and out into the cool September night. She could already smell the first hints of fall in the air. Pinpoints of light filled the clear sky overhead. She yanked open the 4Runner door and tossed her bag onto the passenger seat and plopped into the driver seat.

She sat without moving, her hand with the keys in her lap. She had never gone to Brad's house without him knowing she was coming. Doubt filled her. What if he was immersed in work and she interrupted? What if he wasn't happy to see her?

She took a deep breath followed by several more. What did it say about her relationship with Brad that she felt nervous about stopping by his place—soon to be her place—unannounced?

She stuck the key in the ignition and started the SUV. She was being ridiculous. Why would Brad marry her if he didn't love her? Of course he'd be happy to see her.

Ten minutes later Cassie made her way up Brad's winding driveway. Mature maples, still fully leafed out and just starting to turn gold and red, hid the house from view until she made the last turn. Relief washed through her when she saw lights on the ground floor. He hadn't gone to bed.

Feeling better about her impetuousness, Cassie rounded the house to the parking space in back. Her headlights swept over a strange car, a late model BMW. The motion-sensor lights mounted on the garage exterior came on and flooded the parking pad.

Damn. Brad had company which meant that he was probably working late again. She never should have come. She parked next to the car and turned off her engine but didn't move. There was no point in trying to sneak away. Brad would've seen her headlights and the exterior alarm would have dinged in the house when the garage lights came on. She was trapped.

Nothing to do now but at least say hi. Maybe she could make an appointment with him to have a talk before the wedding. The thought made her feel angry and then foolish. She was overreacting. Wedding nerves, that's all this was.

She climbed out of her vehicle when she saw the back door open and Brad hurried out.

"Cassie! What's wrong? What happened?" He crossed the parking lot and held out a hand and drew her to him. She saw the worry in his eyes and felt even more foolish.

"I'm sorry," Cassie answered. "Nothing's happened. I have wedding jitters I guess. You've been so busy and I've barely even talked with you. I was beginning to think getting married is a mistake."

Alarm replaced the worry in Brad's eyes. "We are *not* making a mistake. You're right, you just have the jitters." He rubbed his hands up and down her arms and pushed her back so he could look into her eyes.

"I know the preparations have all been a bit

overwhelming for you even with Mother's help." He drew her back into his arms and held her.

"Mother told me you've been a real trooper," he said into her hair. "You'll be fine, I promise. And you'll see more of me than you probably want to on our honeymoon. Just two more weeks. Can you hang on until then?"

Cassie took a deep breath and nodded her head. It felt good to be held. She snuggled closer to Brad's chest. His arms tightened around her. Maybe she *was* just feeling overwhelmed with all the details of a big, fancy wedding.

"I'm sorry I bothered you. I panicked. Are you working?" She pointed toward the BMW.

"Yeah, another late night. I'm sick of the office so we're working here. I'm looking forward to a three week break." Brad loosened his arms and looked down into Cassie's face. "Feeling better?"

"Yes, thank you. I love you."

Brad kissed the tip of her nose. "And I love you. You're going to make a great Mrs. Governor. I need to get back to work or I'd invite you in. You sure you're okay?"

Cassie nodded and stepped away from Brad. "I'm fine. Will I see you before the wedding?"

"Probably not until the rehearsal dinner. I'm working every day and most nights making sure I won't be leaving any loose ends at the office. It's only another two weeks. It'll fly by. I'll try to call you every night. Before you know it you'll be living here with me."

Disappointed that she wouldn't see him but determined not to show it, Cassie pasted a smile on her face. "Okay. I'll see you at the rehearsal dinner." She turned away and climbed back into the 4Runner, winced when the muffler let out a loud burp.

She wouldn't be surprised if Brad bought her a new car for a wedding present. He hated her old SUV. She supposed governor's wives were expected to drive something more classy than a twelve year old vehicle with over two hundred thousand miles on it.

She waved at Brad as she turned and drove away. She felt a little better although she really hadn't gotten what she came for. She had hoped for some snuggle time, time to really talk out her misgivings.

Cassie wondered if she would always come after Brad's work in his life. And now she was back to doubting again, she realized, as she made her way back down the driveway and turned toward her place.

"Is the little woman gone?"

Brad pulled off the polo shirt he had thrown on when he realized it was Cassie in the drive. "Yeah, she's gone. Where were we?"

"Right here, lover boy," Cherise answered. She rubbed her naked body against Brad's chest as she reached for the zipper on his pants.

"Do you think she suspects anything?" she whispered against his ear as she reached inside his pants.

"No." Brad groaned as Cherise grabbed onto his hard length. "Unlike you Cassie is too trusting to believe I'd cheat on her. What did you tell Adam you were doing tonight anyway?"

"I told him that I'm working late, naturally. And I am. I just didn't tell him what I was working on." Cherise nipped Brad's earlobe and pushed his pants off his hips.

"Thanks, Amos," Cassie said as the launch driver handed her the metal dodger frame from the *Alice Rae,* one of the most expensive sailboats at the marina. She set the frame down carefully on the gas dock and grabbed the bag of cushions from Amos.

The *Alice Rae's* owner wanted Cassie to replace the windows in his dodger and recover his cockpit cushions over the winter season. Normally Cassie would have taken only the dodger and left the frame on the boat, but Ian Franklin had already dismantled everything and had it waiting for her.

She couldn't very well tell him to put it back.

The customer was always right and she needed to make this particular customer happy.

Even though it was a relatively small job, getting the job was a major coup for Cassie. The dodger and cushions had been made by the largest, most prestigious canvas shop in Portland. By all rights Ian Franklin should have taken the cushions and dodger back to their original maker.

The fact that Franklin chose Cassie to do the work instead was a declaration that he considered her to be the best. It was a major boost to her confidence. Making a customer of Ian Franklin's caliber happy would also boost her business.

She grinned at Amos as she took the cushions from him. "Thanks, Amos. I'll run and grab a cart to haul these to the shop." She ran lightly up the dock and through the locked gate.

It was a glorious September day and Cassie's favorite time of year. The air was clear and fresh, smelling of fall and salt. Sunlight sparkled off the water and reflected off shiny fiberglass hulls.

Half of the moored boats at the marina had been pulled from the water for the season, leaving only the hardcore boaters. The frenzy of the summer boating season had relaxed into a slower pace.

Cassie waved at Stan. He stood atop a ladder

running a propane flame over the heavy plastic that covered a motor boat. Now that the sailing season was drawing to a close Stan spent half his day shrink-wrapping the boats that were stored outside for the winter.

Neat rows of pulled boats filled half the marina yard, all either covered or waiting for covers. Cassie marveled at how much larger they looked on land compared to when they were in the water.

She selected a cart and headed back toward the gate, reaching it at the same time as two teenagers.

"Well, if it isn't the canvas girl," said the older of the two.

Cassie forced a smile but said nothing. She had seen the brothers several times since the day the younger one had pulled her into his lap on Pauli's launch and still hadn't warmed up to them. They were arrogant and rude and drove their father's cigarette boat like they owned the bay.

She waited for them to go through the gate and followed with her cart. The boys were showing off, punching each other in the arm and stealing glances at Cassie over their shoulders to see if she was watching.

She shook her head in disgust when the older of the two took a pack of cigarettes from his jacket pocket and lit up. He handed his younger brother the lit cigarette and lit another.

Cassie smothered a smile when the younger teen choked and coughed. Fools. She slowed her steps to put more space between them so she wouldn't have to smell the smoke.

They were climbing into Amos's launch when the vision hit. She saw a fireball and pieces of boat flying into the air.

Cassie dropped the cart handle and raced down the dock.

"Amos! Amos wait!" Cassie grabbed the side of the launch.

"Don't take them out to their boat."

"What? What are you talking about? Why on earth not?" Amos frowned at Cassie. The boys glowered at her.

"Because. . . because something terrible is going to happen. I can feel it."

Amos looked at her for a long moment then shook his head. "Let go of the launch, Cassie. I have to do my job."

"Yeah, let go of the launch," repeated the older

brother. "What a whack job. C'mon, Amos. We're in a hurry."

"Amos, please," Cassie pleaded. She could hardly breath. The certainty that something terrible was about to happen pressed on her chest like a cement mooring block.

"It' ll be fine, Cassie. You're just stressed because of the wedding. I'll see you later." Amos gently pried Cassie's fingers off the launch rub rail and backed away from the gas dock.

"Oh God. Oh God." Tears were streaming down Cassie's face as she watched Amos wend his way through the boats to the bright red cigarette boat.

"Cassie? What's wrong?"

Cassie turned toward Pauli. She hadn't heard him come down the dock. "It's Amos. He's taking those two boys out to Daddy's cigarette boat. I saw. I saw the boat blow-up, Pauli. I tried to stop Amos but he didn't believe me."

Pauli looked out at Amos. The boys were climbing on board their father's boat. He shouted at Amos but Amos didn't hear him.

Pauli leaped into the second launch. "Call an ambulance, Cassie. Tell the guys in the shop a powerboat just exploded."

Cassie couldn't tear her eyes away from the

red boat. She saw Amos turn and head back toward the gas dock. "Hurry," she said under her breath. "Come on, Amos. Get out of there."

A big boom shook the air and a large black cloud of smoke filled the area where the cigarette boat had been moored.

She watched the stern of Amos's launch lift into the air and crash back onto the water, sending up spray from both sides. Amos was no longer in the launch.

"Cassie! Call for an ambulance!" Pauli shouted over his shoulder as he goosed the launch's engine.

Cassie pulled her phone from her pocket and dialed nine-one-one as she raced for the mechanic's shop. She passed Stan running for the dock. He grabbed her arm.

"What happened?"

"The red cigarette boat exploded. Pauli's out there in the launch looking for Amos and the two boys." She shook off Stan's hand to run for help, but the two marina mechanics were already running toward the dock. Clancy, an older, quiet man was on his phone.

"Did you see which boat?" he asked Cassie when he drew abreast of her.

"The red cigarette."

Clancy shook his head and repeated the information into his phone, then pocketed it. "That was the office. They'll notify the owner. Was anyone aboard?"

Cassie began to shake. "Yes. The owner's two sons. And Amos was knocked out of his launch. Pauli's out there now trying to find everyone."

Clancy's expression turned grim. "Idiot kids. I'll bet they didn't take the time to vent the fumes. The owner's no better. Doesn't have that beast serviced the way he should. It was an accident waiting to happen."

It took twenty minutes for the ambulance to reach the marina. By then the mechanics had taken their service boat and emptied all available fire extinguishers onto the cigarette boat's burning hull.

Pauli had found Amos treading water, dazed, and pulled him into the launch. Together they located the brothers. Both suffered burns and serious injuries. The younger brother had been knocked unconscious and required CPR.

Cassie watched the ambulance race from the marina yard with its lights and siren going, taking Amos and the boys to the Maine Medical Center in Portland. To her relief the EMTs told her that none of the injuries looked to be life threatening although both boys would carry visible scars.

Beyond the restaurant the remaining hulk of the cigarette boat was being hauled out of the water. The owner of the marina, Frank Haskell, stood talking to two local uniforms. The Harbor Patrol pulled up to the gas dock and two harbor police jumped out and hurried up the dock to join them.

"Amos told me you had a premonition something terrible was going to happen. You tried to warn him. Don't beat yourself up."

Cassie turned to see Pauli standing behind her, his face and clothes black from the sooty smoke.

Reporters were milling around the marina but the locked gate kept them off the dock. Even so, she saw several cameras pointed her way and turned her back to them. She tried and failed to stop the shakes racking her body. She looked at Pauli, tears in her eyes.

"It didn't help though, did it?" she whispered. "Amos didn't believe me."

Pauli reached out and clasped one of Cassie's hands in his. "As long as you resist me nobody will ever believe you, Cassie," he said quietly.

"What do you mean? I don't understand what

you're saying." But somewhere deep inside she did understand. She felt a magnetic attraction to Pauli whenever he was near.

He was right—she denied that attraction. She had to. She was engaged to marry Brad.

"Come sit down. You're shaking." Pauli led her to one of the wooden benches on the back edge of the gas dock and drew her down beside him. He covered the hand he was holding with his free hand and said nothing, merely observed her for a few minutes.

The beautiful bright fall day had dimmed for Cassie. She wanted nothing more than to take a scalding hot shower and crawl into her bed with her cat and pull the covers over her head.

She made herself look at Pauli. His blue eyes were intense with an emotion she didn't want to acknowledge. The look in his eyes made her feel weak and shaky. Made her want to throw herself into his arms. She tried to pull her trapped hand free but Pauli held tight.

"Have you ever heard the story of Apollo and Cassandra?" Pauli asked.

Cassie shook her head. "N-no. What does that have to do with anything?" She tried to pull her hand away again but Pauli kept a tight hold on it.

He ignored her question and leaned back on

the bench, stretched his legs in front of him—just a relaxed man settling in to tell a story.

"Apollo thought Cassandra was the most beautiful woman he'd ever seen," he began. "She was the daughter of King Priam and Queen Hecuba of Troy, you know."

Despite herself, Cassie felt a small smile twitch her lips. "No, I didn't know," she said.

Pauli nodded gravely. "It's true. Apollo was so smitten—"

"Smitten?"

Pauli scowled at Cassie. "Don't interrupt. As I was saying, Apollo was so *smitten* with Cassandra that he had to have her. He hit upon the plan to give her the gift of prophesy to show her how much he loved her."

Pauli felt Cassie stiffen beside him. He watched her carefully as he continued. "Cassandra accepted Apollo's gift but continued to refuse Apollo's offer of marriage. He became enraged and cursed her. He let her keep his gift, but he decreed that no one would ever believe her prophecies until she came to her senses and became his."

Cassie frowned at Pauli. "What does that have to do with me?"

"Think about it Cassandra," Pauli answered

softly. "Pauli is my family's nickname for Apollo. For thousands of years Cassandra and Apollo have been forced to live out this scenario over and over again—me trying to win your heart and you trying to get people to believe your visions."

Cassie scowled. "Don't be ridiculous. I'd certainly know if I was the daughter of the King and Queen of Troy."

"You're a descendent, Cassie. Just like I'm a descendent of Ap0llo. What was your mother's name?"

"Cassandra. But that doesn't mean anything," Cassie hurried to add. "Lots of girls are named for their mothers."

"Uh-huh. Where is your mother now, Cassie?"

"She's dead," Cassie whispered. "She committed suicide when I was very young."

"She committed suicide because she couldn't live with her gift. Like you, nobody believed your mother's visions."

Cassie couldn't breathe. She felt dizzy and numb. Pauli's story was only a story—yet it explained so much. And despite its outlandishness it had the ring of truth to it. She felt pieces of her life sliding into new positions and clicking into place.

"Wait. Someone believed me. What about

Sarah MacDougal? Her mother believed me when I told her that Sarah looked unwell."

"Yes, she did. And do you remember what happened the night before you told Mrs. Mac-Dougal her daughter seemed ill?" Pauli asked softly. "I kissed you for the first time. And you kissed me back. You felt something when I kissed you, admit it."

For a brief moment Cassie felt something hopeful flutter inside her. Then she remembered who and what she was. She shook her head and stomped firmly on that flutter.

"I'm engaged to Brad," she said. "We're getting married in three days. I can't back out now." She pulled her hand free and stood. "There's no place for you in my life other than as a friend, Pauli."

Cassie turned away and ran up the dock.

CHAPTER 17

"Nervous?" Amber grinned at Cassie. They were alone in the small room at the back of the church where the bridal party waited for their cue to begin the walk down the aisle.

"Just think, tomorrow there will be several hundred strangers filling the pews and you will magically morph from Cassandra Brown into Mrs. Brad Farland the Third." Amber's grin grew wider. "I wonder how many newspapers will have photographers waiting for you outside the church?"

Cassie scowled at her friend. "Stop it. You're supposed to be my friend as well as my maid of honor. That means you're supposed to support me, not frighten me."

Amber chuckled as Cassie opened the door a crack and peered at the front of the church. Brad stood in front of the alter with his best man Adam listening to the clergyman and the wedding planner Charlotte had hired. To their far right relaxing against the wall were four ushers, all lawyers who worked with Brad.

No one stood on the bride's side.

The four ushers were originally meant to be groomsmen but Cassie had refused to have bridesmaids. Charlotte had tried to convince Cassie that she needed four bridesmaids to balance out the wedding party but Cassie insisted that her maid of honor was all she wanted. She didn't want four women she didn't know—women chosen by Charlotte—standing with her.

After several heated discussions Charlotte had thrown up her hands and conceded to Cassie's wishes. The groomsmen were demoted to ushers.

Cassie saw her future mother-in-law sitting alone in the front pew on the right side of the church, her back rigid, not a hair out of place. Adam's wife Cherise sat two pews behind Charlotte.

Amber peeked over Cassie's shoulder. "I'm glad Tyler came with me for the rehearsal dinner.

We'd be sorely outnumbered otherwise. Who is that sitting behind your future mum?"

Cassie had to smirk at the idea of Charlotte Farland being called a "mum." "That's the best man's wife, Cherise Perry."

"Huh. She's a looker."

"Yeah. I'm pretty sure she cheats on her husband."

"Really? What makes—"

Before Amber could finish her question the wedding planner raised her voice so Cassie and Amber could hear her. "Okay. This is where we cue the music and the maid of honor makes her way down the aisle. And . . . now."

"See you at the altar," Amber said. She walked in measured steps down the aisle, pretending to be holding a bouquet.

When Amber reached the altar she stepped to the left of the clergyman. The wedding planner adjusted her position and called to Cassie. "Now the bride. Remember to smile."

With her father dead and no other family or older close friend, there was nobody to lead Cassie down the aisle and give her away. She had to make the trip alone.

The altar looked so far away. Tomorrow hundreds of strangers would watch her make this solitary journey. The trip down the aisle would feel endless.

She pushed down the nerves and pasted on a smile, then stepped into the aisle, counting the timing in her head. Her eyes darted to Brad. His eyes twinkled back as he smiled at her. He looked so handsome, so sure of himself.

This would be her last night alone, she told herself as she approached the altar. After tomorrow she would never be alone in the world again.

The rehearsal finished with only minor adjustments from the wedding planner. Everyone left the church for the country club where Charlotte had reserved a private dining room for the rehearsal dinner.

Cassie rode to the club with Brad and Charlotte. She sat in the back seat, grateful for the dark shadows while Charlotte talked non-stop about everything Cassie needed to do the next day, listing the people she wanted Cassie to be especially charming to.

"Mother." Brad broke into Charlotte's litany.

"Have I forgotten somebody?" Charlotte turned her attention to her son.

"Cassie doesn't know who those people are yet. You and I will take her around and introduce her and she'll be charming to everyone. Won't you, honey?" Brad looked at Cassie in the rearview mirror.

She smiled. "I'll certainly do my best." She had the sinking feeling that tomorrow was going to be a very long and trying day. Fortunately it would be followed by a three week honeymoon. Just her and Brad.

Cassie saw Clarissa as soon as she entered the club behind Charlotte. From the expression on Clarissa's face Cassie guessed she was still angry about the comment Cassie had made in the ladies room at the Summer Ball.

Cassie pasted a smile on her face.

"That blonde looks like she wants to stab you with a very sharp knife," Tyler whispered in her ear.

Cassie grabbed his arm. "I'm so glad you both came to the dinner," she whispered back. "Where's Amber?"

"She needed the loo. She should be right along. May I escort you into the dining room?"

Cassie saw that Charlotte had taken Brad's arm. She held out her own to Tyler with a real smile. "I'd be delighted." She genuinely liked the store owner and felt happy for Amber. She had to admit that she also felt relieved to have them with her tonight.

The dark carved paneling warmed the small intimate dining room. Crystal, silver, and white china gleamed in the light of the candelabrum over the table. The four ushers and Adam stood to one side of the room drinking flutes of champagne. A waiter offered champagne to Brad and Charlotte and then Tyler and Cassie as they entered the room.

Cassie smiled and made small talk and wished Amber would hurry up and join them.

Amber was more than ready to join Tyler and Cassie but she was trapped in the ladies room sitting area. She sat in the corner out of sight from the two women in the bathroom and prayed they wouldn't find her there.

From what she heard of their conversation Clarissa and Cherise apparently knew one another. They had been chattering non-stop since entering the ladies room behind Amber.

They hadn't seen her duck into the sitting area to remove her new shoes and rub her sore toes. The two women thought they were alone. Their conversation made Amber feel sick and angry at the same time.

"I can't believe you and Brad have been carrying on an affair without Adam or that bitch Cassandra suspecting," Clarissa said.

The admiration in Clarissa's voice made Amber want to spring from her chair and punch Clarissa's perfect nose. But she stayed hidden, knowing she needed to hear more.

"It's easy," Cherise answered. "Adam works late every night. He's so competitive. Brad is making partner after the wedding and Adam wants partner as well so he stays at the office until midnight. If he calls me while I'm with Brad I tell him I'm working."

"What about Cassandra Brown? Doesn't she suspect?"

Amber's hands tightened into fists when she heard Cherise's scornful laugh.

"She's clueless. Can you believe Brad hasn't had sex with her yet?"

The two women tittered.

"Will you keep seeing Brad after the wedding?" Clarissa asked.

"I don't see why not. We'll probably set up a small apartment so we have a private place to meet."

"Oh, this is delicious," Clarissa said. "I wish I could tell that bitch that you've been screwing Brad. I'd like to see the expression on her face when she finds out."

"If you say anything, Clarissa, I will ruin you, I swear."

"Don't worry. My lips are sealed."

The voices faded and Amber heard the ladies room door close. She waited for several more moments to be sure Cherise and Clarissa were gone, then got up and stood at the washbasin. She looked at her face in the mirror. Her freckles stood out against her too-pale skin and her eyes looked angry.

Amber couldn't believe that Cassie and Brad hadn't had sex before the wedding. What if they were incompatible in bed? What if Brad's kisses didn't excite Cassie? She shuddered at the thought of sharing a marriage bed with someone who didn't make her pulse race the way Tyler did.

Should she tell Cassie what she had overheard? She didn't want to see her friend hurt and learning that Cherise was having an affair with Brad would definitely hurt Cassie.

Cassie was marrying Brad tomorrow. Cassie, who had no family and nobody to look out for her. Marrying into the Farland money would at least mean that if Cassie discovered the affair then she would be well provided for when she divorced Brad.

Mind made up, Amber made her way to the rehearsal dinner.

"There you are," Cassie said when Amber entered the dining room.

Amber spotted Cherise flirting with the group of ushers. Her husband Adam stood talking with Brad. He looked relaxed and innocent of any wrong-doing. Amber pasted a smile on her face and focused her attention on Tyler and Cassie.

The rehearsal dinner took several hours. The food and wine was superb but Cassie tasted very little of it. She sat between Tyler and one of the ushers and listened to the conversations around her, mostly work related.

She learned that the ushers were all young lawyers at Brad's firm. She made a few attempts to learn about the one sitting beside her but he was trying to follow the conversation between Brad and Adam so she quickly gave up.

She couldn't talk about her work of course. Tyler had asked about the boat explosion but he sensed that Cassie didn't want to talk about it and he dropped the subject readily enough. She ate quietly and tried to listen to the others.

The conversation soon turned to politics and Cassie tuned everyone out. She had a feeling she would endure many of these dinners as Mrs. Brad Farland the Third.

CHAPTER 18

THE CHURCH WAS FILLED with people. The dress-maker had helped Cassie into her gown and left to take his seat so he could watch his creation float down the aisle. The hairdresser and makeup artist that Charlotte had hired had done their thing early that morning at Charlotte's spa.

Cassie had been primped and prodded and supposed she looked her best. She tried to shake off the sensation of not feeling like herself. She felt removed from the activity around her, as if she was observing herself in a dream.

She heard the low murmur of voices on the other side of the door. Hundreds of voices. Hundreds of people she didn't know. Her stomach clenched. She just needed to get through the next five or six hours and everything would be okay.

Cassie looked up and saw her friend Amber watching her. Amber wore a bronze gown that showed off her coloring. She looked terrific.

She also looked worried.

"You look like I feel," Cassie joked. "You'll do fine."

"It's not that," Amber said.

Cassie frowned. "Is something wrong, Amber?" She reached out and placed a hand on her friend's arm. "Everything is good with you and Tyler, right? You look so good together."

Amber managed a weak smile. "Everything's great with me and Tyler." She had spent a restless night wondering what to say to Cassie—if anything. Several times she had picked up the phone and started to dial Cassie's number, only to hang up.

Finally she had told Tyler what she'd overheard at the club. He'd been angry with Brad for treating Cassie so shabbily and adamant that Amber tell Cassie before she made a terrible mistake. Cassie deserved to know the truth, he'd argued. Then she could make the decision whether to marry Brad or not.

Tyler had also insisted that Amber tell Cassie

in person, not over the phone. She had driven to Cassie's apartment early that morning but Cassie had already left for the spa.

"Amber? If it isn't Tyler then what is it? You're worrying me. Tell me. Maybe I can help."

Amber shook her head. Cassie saw tears glisten in her green eyes. Whatever was bothering Amber was serious.

"Tell me," she demanded.

Amber took a deep breath. "Last night when I was in the ladies room at the club I sat in the sitting area to rub my sore feet. My new shoes hurt."

Cassie said nothing and waited. She knew shoes weren't the problem.

"Adam's wife Cherise and Clarissa came into the bathroom and were talking." Amber swallowed the lump in her throat. She didn't want to say the words.

"They were talking about the affair Cherise has been having with Brad for the last couple months," she finished in a rush.

Cassie frowned. "*What?*" She couldn't have heard Amber right. "What?" she repeated.

Now that it was out Amber found her anger again. She shook her maid of honor bouquet at Cassie. "Brad has been boinking that skank Cherise for the last couple months and apparently has no plans to stop. I heard her tell Clarissa that they were going to find a small apartment where they could do the dirty deed after the wedding."

Cassie stood frozen. Her brain couldn't quite comprehend Amber's words.

"Brad—*my Brad* has been having an affair with Adam's wife Cherise while refusing to sleep with *me*?"

"That's about the size of it."

Cassie glared at her friend. "Why didn't you tell me last night? Why wait until now?"

Amber scowled. "I wanted to. I picked up the phone to call you a bunch of times last night but I couldn't do it. Tyler said you needed to know so I went to your place early this morning but you'd already left."

She shook her bouquet at Cassie again. It was starting to look a little bedraggled from the abuse. "I was going to call you when you weren't there, but then I thought that if you were married at least you'd get some of the Farland money when you discovered what a cad Brad is and divorced him."

Cassie huffed out a harsh breath. "Thanks, but if I promise to love, honor, and obey 'til death do us part then I will do just that. And I certainly wouldn't marry for money."

Cassie gave Amber a brief hug. "Thank you. You've just saved me from a miserable life." She hugged Amber again and opened the door to the church.

"Where are you going?"

"To break off my engagement," Cassie shot over her shoulder as she left the room.

"This oughta be good," Amber said to no one and leaned against the doorway to watch.

Cassie strode down the church's center aisle, ignoring the curious expressions on the faces of the strangers filling the pews as she passed them. Conversations died down to soft murmurs and then stopped altogether.

She saw Charlotte turn in the front pew to see why the church was suddenly silent. Charlotte looked startled to see Cassie coming down the aisle and frowned at her. She started to rise from her seat.

"Sit." Cassie said loudly, and pointed at Charlotte.

Cassie knew she was messing up Charlotte's carefully orchestrated wedding production. Too bad. She wondered if Brad's father had carried on with other women while married to Charlotte. It wouldn't surprise her to learn that Brad Farland *the Second* had been unfaithful.

She looked for Cherise and found her sitting on the aisle two pews behind Charlotte, staring at Cassie with a smirk on her face. She'd deal with the skank later.

Cassie came to a halt at the bottom of the altar steps and looked up at Brad. "Tell me the truth," she said in a ringing voice. She knew everyone behind her was straining to hear. Well, she'd make damn sure everyone knew that Brad Farland III was slime.

"Tell me the truth," she repeated. "Have you been having an affair with Adam's wife Cherise?"

Brad's eyes widened. He made a movement with his hand trying to get Cassie to lower her voice.

"Truth, Brad. Simple yes or no." Cassie folded her arms across her chest and tapped her foot.

"Can we take this somewhere private?" Brad hissed.

"So it's true." Cassie gave Brad a disgusted look. "I'm not going anywhere with you. And I'm certainly not going to marry you. You use people, Brad. You don't deserve to be governor."

She turned away and heard flesh strike flesh. When she turned back she saw Adam standing over Brad, his hands clenched into fists. Brad looked up at Adam from the floor, his left eye already swelling. Good. A black eye was the least Brad deserved.

"You bastard." Adam pulled Brad up by his shirt. "You've been screwing my wife. I thought we were friends." Instead of punching Brad again he tossed him back to the floor. "You're not worth it."

Cassie smiled at Adam and turned to make her way out of the church. When she drew abreast of Cherise she stopped and pointed at her, pleased to see that Cherise no longer wore a smirk. Her face looked pale and her eyes were frightened.

"If anyone cares, this is the skank who's been cheating on Brad's best man," Cassie said in a clear voice. "Her name is Cherise Perry. She's an attorney at Petti and Flowers. If you're looking for an honest attorney you don't want to hire her."

Cassie ignored the eager whispers as she headed for the rear of the church. She heard the dull roar of a powerful engine and saw a sleek black motorcycle pull up to the open double wide door of the church.

Her vision! But instead of the catastrophe she had originally seen, this was the perfect ending.

Her heart lifted. She knew who was on that motorcycle. Pauli had come for her. Cassie picked up the skirts of her gown and sprinted toward the doors. She stopped briefly to hug Amber and thank her again, then ran outside to begin the life she had always been meant to live.

CHAPTER 19

Pauli and Cassie were married at the family villa in the Italian Alps where Zee and Pandora's union had taken place.

Cassie liked Pauli's large family altho she had to admit that it felt somewhat intimidating to be partying with gods, demi-gods, and the mortals who hung with them. She especially liked Zee and Pandora and was touched by the obvious closeness of the half-brothers.

Pauli's twin sister, Artemis, treated Cassie with a great deal of suspicion when they first arrived, but once Pauli convinced her that he loved Cassie, Artemis accepted her new sister-in-law with a warm embrace and welcomed her to the family.

Pauli loved her. The still fresh wonder and amazement over that fact still had the power to take Cassie's breath away. She didn't think she'd ever grow used to it.

"Come on, Cass, we're going to miss the start of the games." Amber grabbed Cassie's hand and tugged. She and Tyler had been thrilled to attend Cassie and Pauli's wedding.

Tyler was combining the trip with a shopping expedition led by Pauli's mother Leto. His excitement when he told Cassie about the quirky finds he'd bought for his shop in Portland had made her smile. She'd be willing to bet that Tyler's shop would soon become an important destination for tourists visiting Portland.

"What games?" Cassie followed her friend.

"Pandora says the men always compete whenever there's a family gathering. I heard her tell Zee that he better let his father win 'cause she wasn't ready for him to be head god yet."

Amber's eyes sparkled. "Can you imagine being married to the head god? Wow. Just think, if you had married that dickhead Farland we'd have missed out on all this."

"Yes. I made a scene in a church filled with hundreds of people just so we could come to Italy and hang with the gods."

Amber laughed and hugged Cassie. "And I for one am very grateful."

Later that night Cassie lay in her marriage bed with her cheek on Pauli's chest and his arm holding her close.

"Happy?" he asked softly.

"Yes. I never thought I could hold this much happiness. I only wish my father had lived to see me married."

Pauli's arm tightened. "I'm sorry he couldn't be with you. I hope you will consider my family your own. They have certainly taken you into their hearts just as I knew they would."

Cassie sighed and ran her hand lightly over Pauli's taut abdomen. "Your family is wonderful. Zee's mother Hera even gave me some pointers on how to control my visions and get the most from them. It made me feel . . normal. Like a normal woman."

Pauli placed his free hand on Cassie's hip and rolled her on top of him. He looked into her warm brown eyes and felt a great peace. This was the woman he was meant to be with, the woman he was meant to have a family with.

He held her face between his hands and kissed her forehead, nose, and lips. "One thing we haven't had a chance to discuss. . . "

"Yes?"

"How do you feel about children?"

"I love them. Why?"

"Well, as you can see I have a very large family. Everyone is expected to help keep it that way." He smiled slowly, his deep blue eyes hot on hers.

Cassie leaned her head down and stopped just shy of Pauli's lips. "I think we can do our part," she whispered and sank into the kiss.

Turn the page for the first chapter of Artemis, the third book in the Romancing a God series.

YA MYSTERY

Gypsy Gold

Dark Horse

Desert Star

STEAMPUNK

Steampunk Heart

JUNKYARD DOG SCI-FI SERIES

Junkyard Dog

Kraken Blues

Deadly Cargo

Ruby City

Double Cross

Spider Silk

Rose Sunstone

New Earth

Red Mist

Ghost Ship

Bolkarus Station

Omega Lab

Mars Base

Junkyard Dog Collection Books 1-3

Junkyard Dog Collection 2 Books 4-6

Junkyard Dog Collection 3 Books 7-9

Junkyard Dog Collection 4 Books 10-13

UPHEAVAL SERIES

Slow Walk

Edge of Reality

Solstice Moon

Upheaval Series Collection

ROMANCING THE GODS

Pandora

Cassandra

Artemis

Andromeda

ROMANCE

Twisted Sister

DESTINATION DEATH MYSTERY SERIES

Stalked in Paradise

Masked in Paradise

Frozen in Paradise

Buried in Paradise

ABOUT THE AUTHOR

Charley Marsh's curiosity drove her to climb mountains, canoe rivers, and explore caves and wilderness areas from Maine to California. She's been shot at, caught in a desert flash flood, and almost drowned off the Maine coast. Once she tobogganed down a 5,000+ foot mountain.

Life is always an adventure if you have the right attitude.

Charley never set out to be a storyteller, but looking back on the elaborate lies she made up as a troubled teen she can see that she always had the makings. Now, in the immortal words of Lawrence Block, she happily "makes up lies for fun and profit."

If you would like information regarding Charley's new releases or simply want to contact Charley visit:

https://charleymarshbooks.com/

www.ingramcontent.com/pod-product-compliance
Lightning Source LLC
Chambersburg PA
CBHW070920190726
48292CB00004B/1042